Heartland Joy

A Heartland Cowboy Christmas Book One

Jessie Gussman

Published By: Jessie Gussman

Acknowledgments

Cover art by Julia Gussman
Editing by Heather Hayden
Narration by Jay Dyess
Author Services by CE Author Assistant

Listen to a FREE professionally performed and produced audio-book version of this title on Youtube. Search for "Say With Jay" to browse all available FREE Dyess/Gussman audiobooks.

Contents

Chapter 1

How long had it been since he'd ridden on a grocery store cart?

Shawn Barclay watched as an older teenage boy, or possibly a young man in his early twenties, started at the back end of the parking lot, pushing his cart with one foot on the back bar and one foot pushing like a skateboard, gaining momentum as he hurled across the blacktop.

Shawn held his watermelon under one arm and slowed his stride just a little, grinning.

It was a good thing he'd bought a watermelon, or he might have been tempted to join the dude in a shopping cart race.

He and his brothers had done that more than once growing up, much to his mother's disapproval.

Never in a lot that had been so busy, though.

It was unseasonably hot for October. October in Arkansas anyway.

That's where Shawn had grown up.

But for Iowa?

It was his first day here, and he wasn't sure.

Still, the watermelon would be a great lunch before he found the farm where his parents wanted him to help out over the winter.

The dude with the shopping cart must have done it a time or two before because somehow, he managed to tilt the cart up on one wheel and spin it in an entire circle before it thumped back down and he gave it two more giant pushes with his leg.

Shawn's smile had slipped, however, because a woman, her cart laden with groceries, hurried out of the store, glancing at the dark, billowing clouds rolling in from the west.

Shawn didn't think it was going to start pouring in the next five minutes, but maybe the woman wanted to get home and have her groceries unloaded before the storm started.

Regardless, she wasn't paying attention to the dude on the cart, and the dude certainly wasn't paying attention to her.

He'd developed a little bit of an audience, and he seemed to be playing to them, swerving the cart into screeching S turns before he grinned at the folks standing and watching, then shoved with two more big pushes before he rode the cart with both hands in the air.

It was at that point that the lady hurrying out of the store must have heard the commotion and jerked her head around in the direction of the dude on the cart barreling toward her.

Maybe she could have avoided a collision if there hadn't been so many groceries in her cart.

She yanked back on the handle; her frame, though slight, seemed strong and agile.

Iowa was a lot different than Arkansas. Flat for one.

The sky was huge, not hidden by any mountains and very few hills. It was farm country, just like Shawn had come from in Arkansas.

Still, it wasn't home, although there were plenty of people in Arkansas just like this woman in front of him: short, no-nonsense haircut, and despite her predicament of being directly in the way of a barreling cart, she definitely wasn't a maiden in distress, seeing the danger and working to avoid it rather than standing like a deer in headlights, waiting to be rescued.

Still, Shawn could never resist even the idea of a damsel in distress, and he ran forward, dropping his watermelon and grabbing hold of her cart, adding his weight to hers for a second or two while the dude riding toward them, finally aware there were other people in the parking lot, put all of his skills to work to try to avoid the imminent collision.

Maybe if Shawn had gotten there just a second earlier, they might have been successful.

As it was, he hit the front right corner of the cart, jerking it with enough force to spin it and throw the woman and Shawn to the right as the cart swung left.

Shawn might have been better off if he hadn't run to help at all, since he ended up landing on top of the woman, getting both feet tangled in the wheel of the cart, and tumbling to the ground.

"That didn't quite go the way I planned," Shawn muttered as the woman moved under him, grunting just a little.

He unwound his long legs from hers and stood, the jeans he wore protecting his legs from any scrapes, although the palms of his hands burned from catching himself on either side of her.

The lady, on the other hand, didn't make it out quite so well. He could see a scrape on her upper arm and some blood on her wrist. As she rolled over, both of her knees were scraped because of the knee-length skirt she wore.

He offered his hand. She grasped it, and he pulled as she leaned back against it, wedging her feet on the blacktop and stretching to her feet.

"Thank you," she said, glancing at her cart which had stopped a few feet away, before brushing herself off.

The dude who'd hit them came back with his hands in his pockets, having gotten his cart stopped. "I'm sorry about that, Bridget. I didn't see you there."

"It's okay, TJ," the lady said, looking at the brush burn on her arm which had to be burning, even though it wasn't bleeding profusely.

Shawn did a double take at the woman. "It's okay?" he asked incredulously. "The dude just ran into you. Aren't you...like, angry?"

The woman turned her head and narrowed her eyes, almost like she was angry at him for suggesting that she should be angry. "Why would I be angry? No one got hurt." She moved her eyes over him from top to bottom. "You look like you're fine...are you okay?" She asked that last question like it just occurred to her that he might have been hurt.

"I'm fine, but you're all scraped up. It's because the guy was careless. Showing off." Shawn swept his eyes around the parking lot where TJ's admirers had been gathered. They'd dispersed now, and no one was in sight.

"He was just having fun, and I'm glad he was able to." She gave Shawn another side glance before she moved her gaze to TJ. It wasn't a look of affection, exactly, but more the look of someone who'd known someone for a really long time. "How's your mother doing?"

TJ already looked abashed, and now his eyes went to the ground. "Not good. I'm here to pick up her prescription for more painkillers," he mumbled. Then he jerked his head at Shawn, who tilted his head ever so slightly in return, still jacked that the dude seemed to be getting away with being irresponsible and running into people and no one seemed to care. TJ pulled his hand out of his pocket and waved it in the lady's direction. "I'd better go get it. Sorry again," he murmured as he strode away.

The lady let out a deep breath, then turned to her cart, grasping the handle with one hand while she shook the hand with the scrape on her palm a little before touching the cart with it.

"You probably have some stones pushed up in there, and your knees are scraped up too. Do you have someone who can look at it?"

Shawn should just leave. The lady had been very clear that she was not upset, and she wasn't going to make a big deal about it.

He appreciated the lack of drama. Some people made big deals out of everything, and it got tiring. But honestly, that dude should be held accountable. He could hurt someone else if he didn't stop being so careless.

Of course, more than once, Shawn had been the one riding a cart in the parking lot, and he had been enjoying watching the guy until he had run into the lady.

If he'd run into someone though, he would have spent a lot more time apologizing and making sure she was okay. But that dude acted like he couldn't wait to get away from her.

"I'll be fine. I do appreciate your concern. But TJ's had a pretty hard summer since his mom and sister were in an accident. His sister didn't make it, and his mom is having a difficult recovery."

Shawn pursed his lips, feeling bad for TJ but not bad enough that he wanted to give him a free pass to run into anyone with a shopping cart.

Still, if the lady wasn't angry, he would try to hold his own temper. "Oh. I see. I'm sorry, I guess you have the advantage of being a hometown girl. I'm new."

"I know. I should have introduced myself. I'm Bridget Rallings." She held out her hand, then kinda shrugged and looked apologetic. "You probably don't want to shake since I'm bleeding."

Shawn took the hand she offered, but instead of shaking, he turned it over and cradled it in his. "There are a couple of stones in there." He looked up. "You never answered my question about whether or not you have someone to help you get them out."

"They'll work their way out. I'll clean them good when I get home." Her words wobbled a little, and she swayed, taking her hand out of his and grabbing a hold of the cart.

"Are you sure you're okay?" he asked. "If you hit your head, I didn't see it." His eyes scanned her body, looking for a bump he might have missed.

"I thought I was. My head doesn't hurt at all. I just had a little dizzy spell."

He glanced at the clouds. They were boiling on the western horizon but didn't seem to be coming any closer, although there was an occasional gust of wind to dispel the heat that beat down from the sun and radiated out from the black macadam.

"Come on. I'll push your cart. Tell me where your car is. Maybe you can sit down on the bumper for a minute."

Her car wasn't far away. They passed the watermelon he'd dropped as they walked toward it.

"As soon as I get you settled, I'm going back to grab that. That was my lunch," he said, humor in his voice, as she walked slowly beside him, allowing him to push her cart but not having any more wobbles.

"I'm sure I'm fine. I don't know what came over me. I guess I just lost my balance for a minute," she said, almost seeming embarrassed that she wasn't completely strong.

She got her key out and opened the trunk as they walked toward it.

"Do me a favor and sit there on the bumper for a minute. I'll be right back." He waited for her to sit before he turned and jogged back toward his watermelon.

It was cracked, and there was a puddle of juice on the parking lot underneath it.

He picked up the watermelon, careful to hold it so he wouldn't get the sticky liquid on his hands. He had every intention of helping the lady unload her groceries into her car. But as he turned, he could see she was already back on her feet and unloading her cart herself.

He had a feeling he might not be wanted, but he couldn't just walk away, so he walked over, laying his watermelon back down on the ground beside her car. He reached into her cart, pulling out several bags.

"Is there a certain way you want these?"

"No. I didn't get any bread today, and we have our own chickens, so everything else can be put wherever," she said, humor in her voice, which was a little friendlier than she'd been before. But still reserved. "Although these bags here"—she indicated the bags in the front basket of her cart—"are for Matilda, and I'd like to keep them toward the back."

He didn't say anything more but helped her with the rest of it. As she was putting the last bag in, she either lost her balance or had another dizzy spell because her body shuddered and she fell forward. Her shoulder hit the side of the SUV.

"Are you okay?" he asked, pushing the cart away and coming to her side, putting his steadying hand on her shoulder as she straightened.

"I think it's just the heat. Maybe I turned too quickly. I feel fine."

She sighed a little, and he felt compelled to say, "How about you sit down for a minute? I'll share my lunch with you." His eyes crinkled, although he was only half joking. He didn't think there was anything seriously wrong, but sometimes a person just needed a few minutes to recover. He thought that was what was going on here, but in case not, he preferred she not get in her car and drive just yet.

His oldest sister, a surgeon, might have a different take, and if he felt like he needed a professional opinion, he wasn't afraid to text her.

He had time before the farmer he was going to see was expecting him, and while he had zero intention of getting involved with anyone here in Iowa, he wasn't opposed to making friends.

He wasn't going to be staying long enough for anything more.

Chapter 2

B ridget waited so long to reply, Shawn thought she was going to turn him down. But then she said, "Okay." It was hesitant, and she almost looked shy as she looked at him from under her lashes and said, "But I can't stay long. I have to drop off Matilda's groceries and pick my kids up from school."

Immediately, his eyes went to her left hand. No ring. He almost sighed. He'd be concerned about and would have helped anyone. But he probably wouldn't have asked just anyone to share his watermelon. He didn't want to be sitting on the back of someone else's wife's vehicle sharing watermelon with her. No matter how innocent his intentions.

Although, he had to admit he found this woman compelling for some odd reason. He certainly would not mind being friends with her.

Picking the watermelon up, he pulled his pocketknife out of his pocket and used it to slip in the crack and finish the job of halving it.

"You're obviously from around here, if you're picking your kids up at school," he said by way of starting a conversation while he took half of the watermelon and set it aside, focusing on the other half.

"Yep. I've lived in Prairie Rose all my life." Her words sounded a little sad. Forlorn, even.

"Don't you like it here?"

"I love it," she said without hesitation.

"You just sounded a little...like maybe you weren't happy living in Prairie Rose."

"Well, actually, I live on a farm outside of town. So I don't really live in town." She lifted a shoulder and seemed to shake herself a little. "But I love it here. It's gorgeous. The wide-open sky that stretches from horizon to horizon. And there's a sense of pride. Crops everywhere; we feed the nation. It gives you a sense of purpose and makes you feel like you're contributing something necessary and good to society."

"Spoken like a farm girl."

"Yeah. But I think the townspeople feel it too. Because obviously, they help us. We buy our groceries here. Go to church here. Educate our kids. We all work together, so even if they're not directly contributing to the growing of the crops, they help us so that we can."

"I've never actually thought about it that way. But you just described the sense of community that permeates the heartland of this country beautifully. Everybody works together, respecting each other and appreciating each other. There's a sense of pride about what you do."

"You must be from a small town," she said, taking the watermelon he gave her and murmuring, "Thank you for sharing your lunch with me."

"I am. From a small town. And you're welcome. It's not much for lunch. If I'd known I was going to be sharing it, I might have gotten something a little more substantial."

"You actually did just go into the grocery store to buy watermelon for lunch?"

He held up his hand. "Guilty."

"Then you must be passing through."

"Actually, I just came up from Arkansas. I'm going to be staying for a while. Not permanently. But I'm doing a favor for my dad."

"Arkansas?" Her brows furrowed, and she narrowed her eyes a bit.

The watermelon was sweet and good. Unexpected for this late in the season. He finished chewing and swallowed while he figured that maybe she had heard about him coming. He knew how small towns were. Everybody knew everything about everyone else.

She might even be able to give him a heads-up about the person he was supposed to be meeting. A friend of his dad's.

"That's right. Maybe you've heard of me. I haven't talked much to the people I'm going to be helping. A man named Jeffrey Bolton. He's a crop farmer, although he also has a laying house."

"Yeah. I've heard of him." She looked like she'd lost her appetite and stared at the watermelon in her hand like it had turned into a snake.

"Aren't they good people?" It was the only thing he could think of to ask.

She tilted her watermelon, and one side of her lips pulled back. "I guess. They're honest anyway. And you should get a paycheck when you're promised it. The farm isn't as prosperous as it used to be."

"Why do I feel like there's something you're not telling me?" he asked, seeing no reason to beat around the bush. Suddenly he wasn't as interested in his own watermelon, and he'd planned to eat the whole thing.

"I guess some people just say the farm is cursed," she said, the tightness around her lips even more pronounced.

"Cursed?" He grunted. "In what way?"

He didn't believe any of that garbage. There were spirits; he definitely believed in that. The Bible said so. But they weren't stronger than God, and he wasn't going to live in fear of them.

"Seems like every male that lives on the farm dies." She tilted her chin and almost looked as though she were bracing herself for something.

"Really?" He'd never heard of such a thing. "So there've been a couple of accidents on the place?"

Farm accidents were not unheard of. They were actually expected, although, of course, they were tragedies, each and every one.

But farming was a dangerous profession. Heavy equipment,
chemicals, moving parts and pieces, and work that had to get done,
like, yesterday.

But there was nothing Shawn would rather do. The land called
to him, and he knew without a shadow of a doubt he was meant to
live on it, make his living from it, doing an honest day's labor. Not
that there was anything wrong with anything anyone else wanted
to do with their life, but as for him, he was born to be a farmer.

"Every male that lives on the farm ends up dying. On the farm."
Her look was almost challenging as she stared at him steadily. Her
words weren't exactly ominous. They were stated as fact.

"That's odd. Since I'm supposed to talk to Jeffrey. That's a male.
And he lives on the farm."

"That was my dad."

He was able to catch the "was" in her words before he opened his
mouth. Shock tore through him. The farm that she claimed was
cursed, was hers.

"He passed away earlier this year from injuries he sustained in
the accident that killed my husband two years ago."

Shawn stared at her, trying to think of what his dad had told him.

He could have sworn he said he talked with his friend. Maybe he
had come earlier this year.

"I'm so sorry about the loss of your father and husband."

"That was my second husband." And now there was no doubt to
the challenge in her eyes. "My first husband passed away. On the
farm."

Shawn stared at her, trying to keep his eyelids from fluttering.
So help him, there was a part of him that wanted to get up and
walk away. Find his own vehicle and drive back to Arkansas. He
hadn't wanted to leave his home state. He definitely hadn't wanted
to leave his family. Everyone he knew and loved lived around the
town of Mistletoe.

He'd already lost his birth parents in a car accident. His siblings and his adoptive parents were all he had left.

But his dad asked him to move to Iowa and help a family here. Friends.

He hadn't mentioned this friend was dying.

He also hadn't mentioned that his friend had a daughter who was unmarried.

Shawn's lips tightened a little, wondering whether he'd been set up.

His parents always meant the best for each of their children, and he knew his siblings were glad that their parents had meddled in their love lives. They were all happily married. All, except him.

He thought he'd escaped his parents' matchmaking, thought they knew that he was too much of a goofball to ever be attractive to a woman.

The kind of goofball who bought a watermelon at the store and called it lunch.

Still, he wasn't going to let Bridget's news intimidate him. Obviously, she was sensitive about it.

But he supposed his goofball exterior had always hidden a compassionate nature that wasn't always considered manly.

He let it out now. "It sounds to me like you've been through a lot of loss. You and your children. That has to be hard."

She blinked, obviously not expecting his compassion. Maybe she'd been expecting him to find an excuse and run.

It hadn't been too hard to put that part of him down.

The part of him that rose to a challenge, the part of him that fought for the underdog, the part of him that couldn't not help someone when they needed it; they were all so much stronger than the cowardly part.

"That's not usually what people focus on," she said, not sounding bitter. She looked at the watermelon she held with renewed interest and took a bite. He picked up the last piece of the first half and decided he wasn't going to let anything take his appetite either.

Not even the convoluted puzzle his parents had presented him with.

"You're the only adult on the farm?"

"I am."

"Then I guess I'm going out to meet you."

"I guess you are. But I just told you everything you need to know."

"Really?" He grunted again, because she didn't get it. "I didn't hear anything about crops, how big the farm is, how many acres. I know you have a laying house, and you didn't mention my duties, what you're going to need for me to do."

"I guess you didn't understand. All the men on the farm die."

"Everybody's gonna die sometime. And sometimes, God puts people through trials. But the idea that every man on the farm is going to die on the farm is ridiculous, and I'm not scared." He started cutting the second half. "You want more?"

She laid her rind down beside his on the ground and held out her hand. "It's a good one."

"Takes a certain knack to pick a good watermelon."

"Or luck."

"I don't believe in luck. You make your own luck. And usually that's through hard work and perseverance and determination." He laughed without humor. "And being careful, apparently."

"My dad was being careful. He was turning left into the farm lane, and the car behind him couldn't stop. It pushed him in front of the path of an oncoming truck. My husband was killed instantly. My dad lingered."

"That's good. Your dad lingered long enough to talk to my dad, who sent me to help you. Sounds like you need it."

"You just don't get it."

"Don't get what?"

"Didn't you see TJ couldn't wait to get away from me?"

"He was embarrassed to hit you. He's a grown man riding a shopping cart in the parking lot." Shawn allowed a little derision into his voice, but then he had to add, "I have to admit I've done that a time or two. Although, I've never run into anyone. And it's been at least, oh, I don't know, a good year and a half since I've done it."

As he hoped, she smiled at his small attempt at humor. He thought the poor woman actually believed that bunk about this curse.

"He was probably thanking his lucky stars I didn't kill him."

"If he had died, it would have been his fault." Shawn said that in a tone that allowed for no argument.

"I don't think the town would agree with you."

"I thought we were just talking about what a great thing a small town is."

"TJ was the only person in town who was brave enough to ask me out on a date in the last year. I went, not necessarily because I have feelings for TJ but because I thought it would be nice to get out. I don't think a single person smiled at us, and I know at least four people took TJ aside when he got up to use the restroom during our meal and told him that he'd better steer clear of me."

"That's crazy. I can't believe they blame you for a car accident."

"My first husband died when he was helping put on the annual Christmas firework show that we always had at our farm. It's sponsored by the town, but the farm is where we always had it. One of the fireworks malfunctioned and blew up on the ground. He died immediately."

"Again, sorry for your loss. I think you should have the town rallying around you to support you, not warning people away from you."

"Well, they're going to do it to you."

"They can do it all they want to. I told my dad I'd come out here and help you. I'm going to do what I said I was going to do. And I have no plans on dying anytime soon, but I'm not afraid of death." Maybe those were strong words—tough. But he meant them. Death wasn't something to be feared or avoided like it was the worst thing that could ever happen to a person.

"Everyone's afraid of death. We're supposed to be."

"Maybe, but I don't think it should have the prominent place it does. People should be afraid of being selfish. Or afraid of ignoring their neighbor in need. Or afraid of hurting other people by being unkind to them," he said, thinking about the townspeople who had made this woman feel like she was causing the death of the people dear to her. How awful it must be to lose so many family members. But then to have the townspeople act like they blamed you for it. That was unbelievable. "Death happens to everyone. We definitely shouldn't seek it out. We need to live the best life we can with what we've been given, both in body and in physical and mental abilities, but realize that this is not our final home. I don't know why we act like it is."

"Are you a preacher?" she asked, finishing her slice of watermelon and setting the rind down with his.

He'd almost finished the second half, but he held it up and she nodded, so he sliced another piece off for her.

"My dad is." He didn't get into the fact that he was adopted or that his birth parents had died. It was too complicated, and Race and Penny were just like parents to him. He knew they loved him just as much as his birth parents had.

"You must take after him," she said almost dryly.

"My whole family would laugh at that. I'm probably the least like my dad of all my brothers."

"Really? I find that hard to believe."

"As hard as I find it to believe that you actually believe this whole curse business. And that this town has pretty much convinced you that you're responsible for the deaths of your husbands and family. I may have to go strangle someone. Not exactly preacher thoughts." He didn't hide much of the anger that wanted to come out in his voice.

He figured he'd probably convinced her.

"Maybe you're safe. You're not actually related to me. Or married to me."

He finished his watermelon and shook his head. She was a tough woman. She had so much loss, and yet she was still going. He admired her reaction to the cart barreling toward her. She didn't scream, and she didn't drop her own cart and run. She tried to fix the situation. She hadn't fussed about the cuts and scrapes on her arms and knees, and she sat and ate her watermelon with her hands.

She was a down-to-earth, small-town girl. The kind of girl a man would be proud to be beside. The kind of woman who would give just as much as she took and would grow old with her husband. Unless he died.

What a crock of baloney.

"Thanks for the watermelon. I need to go."

"I don't want to keep you. Is it okay if I mosey out to the farm?"

"Of course. It'll be about an hour, maybe a little less, until I get there."

"That's great. Talk to you then."

He gathered up his watermelon rinds while she closed the back of her car and gave him a last glance before she got in and drove away.

Did his dad know about the curse? His dad wouldn't believe it any more than he did. But maybe Shawn needed to give him a call this evening. He had a few bones he wanted to pick with him.

Chapter 3

B ridget pulled in front of Miss Matilda's house, still thinking
about the stranger she just met.

Shawn.

The son of a friend of her dad. Not a very great connection.

When she'd talked to Mr. Race about him sending some help for
her, Mr. Race had said he knew someone who had just sold his
farm, who loved farming, and who was completely trustworthy.

It had been her wrong assumption that had led her to believe that
if a man was selling his farm, he was old enough to retire and was
willing to postpone that retirement for a bit to help the daughter
of a friend of a friend.

Obviously, her assumption had been way, *way* off.

She got out of her car and went back, opening the trunk and
digging through for the five bags that were Miss Matilda's.

After the incident with the shopping cart, she was still feeling a
bit shaky, and she had to admit she was a little disconcerted by
Shawn's presence as well.

Not because he was devastatingly handsome necessarily, but
there was just a way about him. A deepness to his look. A consideration.

Of course, he was good-looking in a rugged, workingman kind
of way. He definitely looked good in his jeans and T-shirt.

And she liked his quirkiness—who buys a watermelon and eats
it in the grocery store parking lot, calling it lunch?

Most of the guys she knew would have stopped at some fast-food joint, not that there was anything wrong with that. It just made Shawn...different.

She supposed a person was always attracted to other people who were different than what their normal was. It made them stand out. Made them seem new and exciting.

Even though she knew this was a fact, it seemed weird to watch herself actually live it out.

Because it was true. Shawn was different. Not like the men in town, and he drew her interest.

Maybe there was even attraction there. One-sided, of course.

That was probably why she'd worked so hard to push him away talking about the curse.

Although everything she had said was true.

She'd sworn when her second husband had been killed that she wasn't going to marry again.

Marriage wasn't that great anyway. It was just living with a man who thought because he married you, he had the right to tell you what to do.

She could live without that.

Except, when her dad had passed away, it left her with the burden of running the whole farm, which was too much for her.

Bridget shifted the bags and started up the walk.

Miss Matilda had a beautiful front door, with a fall wreath that Bridget had hung herself, getting it from Miss Matilda's attic and putting the summer wreath away.

But she didn't go to the front door. She walked down the narrow path, along the hedge, and to the back where the kitchen door was. Rapping with her knuckles while still holding the bags, she waited for just a few seconds, then grabbed the doorknob with the two fingers that she had free and turned, pushing the door open and calling, "Miss Matilda! It's Bridget. I have your groceries."

"I saw you pull in. I'm coming," the lady said from the living room where she usually sat during the day.

Miss Matilda was no relation to her, but Bridget considered her almost like a grandmother. She'd been a rock through all of the losses that Bridget had suffered. Even though her mobility had declined in the last few years, her brain was as sharp as ever, and she was a fun conversationalist and a great Uno partner when Bridget and her girls came to play games.

But most of all, Miss Matilda had a rock-solid faith, forged through decades of hardship, and the advice she'd given Bridget had been priceless.

Bridget stepped in and used her foot to close the door behind her.

"I was expecting you a while ago," Miss Matilda said as she appeared in the doorway. Osteoporosis had given her a bit of a hunch, and arthritis in her hip and back made her lean forward. But she came into the kitchen with a smile on her face and her brown eyes twinkling, her rosy cheeks brought out by the tight, curly gray hair on her head.

"I had a little mishap in the parking lot, and I stopped to eat a watermelon." Bridget's hands stilled as she pictured Shawn and her sitting on the back of her car, eating watermelon with her hands.

Had she ever done anything like that before in her life?

That was a rhetorical question. She most definitely had not.

"You were eating watermelon?" Miss Matilda's body might be old and failing, but her brown eyes were shrewd. "With a man?"

"Maybe," Bridget said with a little grin. "Okay. I was. A stranger."

"That's good. Maybe you can get to him before the town does."

"Oh no. I would never want him to not know everything there was to know about me, and that includes the curse. I told him all about it."

"Stop calling it a curse. It's not. It's just the Lord giving you trials to grow you and see how you handle them. I believe you've done well, child. You'll see how quickly His hand of blessing turns."

Miss Matilda had reached the table where Bridget had set the bags and was carefully pulling the groceries out and separating them into piles of things that should go in the pantry and things that would go in the refrigerator.

"I'm ready for the blessings, that's for sure. He can shower them down anytime," Bridget said, not really believing He would. For some reason, God had spent most of her adult life angry at her. She wasn't sure exactly what she'd done, but she knew she was being punished for something.

Miss Matilda wanted to call them trials and said they were to form her character and make her stronger, but they didn't feel like trials as much as it felt like getting spanked.

Over and over again.

"Was he cute?" Miss Matilda asked, picking out the carton of eggs and turning toward the refrigerator.

"I think at my age, there is no such thing as cute."

"Oh? So he was your age?"

"I don't know. I didn't ask him. I was too busy telling him to stay away from me. Although, that's going to be kind of hard since...since apparently a friend of my dad's sent his son to help me on the farm, and Shawn is the person. He'll be helping me, I guess."

"You're kidding. You're going to have help on the farm?" Miss Matilda paused with her hand on the handle, her eyes wide. There was also relief on her face. Bridget made a mental note to remember that Miss Matilda not only loved her but worried about her as well.

"For a bit. He was pretty clear that he's not staying. His home is in Arkansas, and he doesn't want to move to Iowa. He's just doing his dad a favor."

She wanted to be grateful. Truly, she did. And she was. Sincerely grateful.

But she kind of wanted someday, somehow, for someone to do something for her because of her. Not because of the farm she lived on or because of doing someone else a favor. Do it because he wanted to make her happy.

Schoolgirl dreams. She needed to grow up.

"Well, I'd say it's nice of him to come. At least you have some help. Although, being that it's October, it would have been better if he'd come in the spring." Miss Matilda put the eggs in the refrigerator and turned back toward the table.

"I'm gonna talk to him whenever I get the kids home from school. I'll probably give him a tour of the farm, and maybe I'll find out then how long he's planning on staying. I guess I kind of thought in my mind that he would be here through next season and do the fieldwork. That's what I really need help with. Although it would be nice to have help in the chicken barn as well."

"Sometimes I think you try to do too much, child."

"I guess you know as well as anyone that you just have to do what you have to do in order to make things work."

"That's true. That's farming. It's not an easy life, although it's a good one."

Miss Matilda knew what she was talking about. She'd been married to her husband, a farmer, for sixty-seven years. When her husband died, her grandsons had taken over the farm, and Miss Matilda had moved into her mother's house in town. The house she'd grown up in.

"I know we talked about that before, and you're right. Where else do you get to have the artwork on your office walls painted by God every morning? And He changes the pictures daily, sometimes even hourly." Bridget took the flour and sugar and dried beans and carried them to the small cupboard, stacking them neatly where they belonged.

"I suppose you can tell Levi and his brothers they won't be renting your fields next year," Miss Matilda said as she picked up the milk and turned toward the refrigerator.

"Once I talk to Shawn and find out what his plans are, I'll definitely be letting your grandsons know immediately. I knew Shawn was coming, although I didn't know when, exactly, and I definitely didn't know he was going to be as young as what he is. But I already told them I wasn't going to commit to renting the fields out until I talked to him." Bridget paused with her hand on top of the can of cream of mushroom soup. "If he's only going to be here for a year, I can't see pulling it away from your grandsons, only to ask them to take them back the next year. I'm not going to do that to them."

"And I'm sure they'll appreciate it, although they understand as well. I know they know that you're going to do whatever you need to do in order to make a living and take care of your girls. I just wish one of them could fall in love with you."

"They're too much like my brothers," Bridget said, and meant it, not taking offense at Miss Matilda's words because she certainly didn't have romantic feelings for the men who'd grown up with her and were more like family than friends.

Although, she felt like Miss Matilda's grandsons might have been influenced a little by the curse as well. They weren't the kind of men who backed down, but the rest of the town was scared to death, and it was hard to stand against that kind of solidarity.

"They're good boys, and I'm glad you've allowed them to take you under their wings a little."

"Pulling them from all the things that they do, because they don't just run the farm," Bridget said, putting the last of the groceries away and turning toward Miss Matilda. "I'm sorry I don't have time to talk. I guess... I guess time just got away from me a little." When was the last time she'd sat and talked to a man...just talked for the fun of it?

"It's okay. It's good for you to sit and smell the roses some. That's what makes life sweet."

"Thanks." She hadn't smelled many roses in her life. "You'll call me if you need anything?" she said as she gave the lady a hug, loving the way her sturdy old arms wrapped around her and reminded her of the few memories she had of her mother before she left.

Her dad didn't talk much about her, and Bridget had lost track of her over the years.

All her father had ever said was that farming was too hard for her and she was made for a softer life.

Bridget hoped she got it. Now. She hadn't understood when she was younger and resented her mother for being weak.

But now that she had the farm to run on her own and she could see just how hard it was…There were always problems, bills to pay, things that went wrong every single day, and of course, in her case, people dying. It seemed like the stress was never-ending. She understood a lot better why maybe her mother couldn't handle it and chose an easier life.

It still didn't make her feel better about her mother choosing easy over her daughter, but that was something she had to learn to live with.

"Tell me how things go with Shawn. And tell your little darlings I said hi," Miss Matilda said as Bridget reached for the doorknob to let herself out.

"I will. I know they miss the summer days and spending time here with you. Robin is still making bread on Saturdays, just like you taught her."

"Good for her. She had a knack for it. Sometimes, that's all it takes."

Bridget waved once more to Miss Matilda and walked out. Was it time for her to sell the farm to move on to an easier life?

Trouble was the farm was mortgaged from the last time grain prices had dipped. It could take a long time to sell and get what they owed out of it.

Still, it might be better just to get rid of it and start a new life somewhere else.

She stopped at her car and looked up at the deep blue Iowa sky.

She didn't want to go anywhere else. This was her home. Her roots were here. The farm had been in her family for generations. She felt like she was letting her ancestors down if she couldn't keep the place going. She had to at least try.

And who was to say that life would be easier somewhere else?

One of her children could get sick. Or she could. They could be in an accident, or a tornado could flatten their new home. Hard lives weren't just confined to a farm. They could be anywhere.

And she wasn't a quitter.

She was an Iowa farmer and proud of it. She would make this work or die trying.

Chapter 4

S hawn had every intention of calling his dad when he got to the farm, but after sitting with Bridget and eating the watermelon and having a bit of insider knowledge since he'd helped her empty her cart and couldn't help but notice that she didn't have any watermelon in her groceries, he decided that he'd go back into the store and grab another one.

She'd enjoyed that one. He didn't question himself too much, but he wanted to see her smiling and happy.

That wasn't something he was going to dwell on, since he wasn't exactly sure where those thoughts came from. He hadn't ever had them before. Buying a watermelon just to make someone smile? Ha. Nope. New territory.

Maybe he just pitied her because she was convinced that she was under a curse. Or maybe he felt bad for her because she had so much loss in her life.

Maybe that was why he wanted to see her smile.

Whatever it was, he ended up buying two more melons because he remembered she had children, and kids usually loved watermelon.

Once he'd done that, he'd been going to head out, but then he saw the barbershop on the edge of town and decided he might as well get his hair cut since there wasn't any rush in getting out to the farm because Bridget wouldn't be there for almost an hour.

There was no line, and the barber had him sit right down in the chair, although two older gentlemen walked in after he did.

Whether or not they needed haircuts, or whether they were just there because they'd seen someone new walk into the barbershop, he wasn't sure. His mom always teased his dad that men gossiped worse than women, and Shawn had quite honestly found that to be true most of the time.

He was pretty sure his mom would put money on the other two gentlemen being there just to get the gossip and not for haircuts.

The barber, destroying the popular stereotype, was a young man and personable.

He would be a good person to ask if he wanted the scoop on the curse that Bridget had talked about. Somehow, he just couldn't bring himself to ask about it. He didn't believe in it and didn't even want to give it the legitimacy of the question.

He was going to avoid the topic completely, but the barber, whose name was Drake, asked him what his business was in town.

"I'm here to help Bridget Rallings on her farm. My dad knew hers." He figured he'd add that last bit because they were sure to ask who he was and how he knew her.

Drake's hands stilled, and then they wavered, and Shawn became concerned about the safety of his eyeballs.

Drake cleared his throat. "Did anyone tell you about the curse?"

"I've already spoken with Bridget. The curse is a crock of buffalo bull."

"Then you must not have heard the whole thing. You know how many men have died out there so far?"

"And every one of them has been close to Bridget. I hope the town has been taking care of her. She's had a lot of tragedy in her life."

"She needs to sell that farm and get away from it. Anyone who's close to her is in danger of dying. Especially men. You do know she has all daughters?"

Shawn hadn't known, and up until that point, he had been liking Drake. Seemed like a good kid with a reasonable head on his shoulders. He had his own opinions and didn't just repeat the talking points of the news. Up until he started talking about Bridget, he hadn't been gossiping.

"And all of her children are healthy," Shawn said, not really wanting for some reason to admit that he'd just met her and didn't even know her children.

He would have a hard time explaining why he was so flat-out determined to defend her.

"Yeah, none of them have died from the curse, either." Drake shook his head.

"If I were you, I wouldn't live on the place."

"That's some good advice, son," one of the men, who had been pretending to read a magazine, said from his chair in the corner. "I wouldn't stay very long if I were you. Sometimes, it takes the curse a little while to work its way in, but sometimes, it acts fast."

"That's true," said the second man, who wasn't even pretending to read a magazine. "She hadn't even been married two years when her first husband died in that explosion." He shook his head, like it was a useless waste of life.

Which it probably was, but it wasn't Bridget's fault.

Before Shawn could speak, Drake spoke again. "That's right, Philip. I don't even think it was two years. Man, and to think I almost dated her in high school. She's a nice girl, but..."

"It's not worth the risk. Now, if you can talk her into moving off the farm, I think you'd be good. Or you can buy it from her and run it yourself," Philip added.

"But I'd stay away from the girl. Even if she does move off the farm. She's just bad luck."

"Men, I appreciate your advice, but I'm going to ask you to stop. I'm not gonna continue to listen to you all speak so terribly about my fiancée."

As soon as the words were out of his mouth, he wanted to shove his tongue back in his throat and plug the hole. Where had they come from?

The barbershop was completely silent. Drake had even quit cutting his hair, and all three men had their mouths hanging open.

He wanted to warn Philip that he was going to lose his dentures, but he was too busy castigating himself for saying something he shouldn't have.

The best time to admit a lie was right away. Before the lie grew legs and had babies.

This was definitely the kind of lie that was going to have babies. Lots and lots of babies.

But he just couldn't bring himself to laugh and say he was just kidding.

Not that he wanted to get married.

Not that he had any special feelings for Bridget. At least not beyond the pity and the slightly protective feeling he had been feeling since finding out the whole town seemed to be against her. She was even against herself.

But he wasn't going to let these people think he was afraid, and he wasn't going to sit here and listen to them say one more word to a stranger in town about how he needed to stay away from her.

She hadn't said she was looking for a man, but whether she was or whether she wasn't, she was never going to find one if this was the greeting that every new man in town got.

Drake was the first to recover. His hands moved, then stopped, then moved again, and Shawn was slightly concerned that he was going to have a bald spot right there on the side of his head.

It was just hair. It would grow back.

"Well...Well...I didn't know that. I didn't even know she was seeing anyone."

"Have I seen you in town before, sonny?" Philip asked, setting his magazine aside and leaning forward. "You look a little familiar."

"I've never been to town before," Shawn said honestly. Now was a great time for his natural honest nature to take back over.

"We have lots of nice girls in town. You might want to pick a different one," the other fella said. "I know we get fed all of this love stuff and everybody thinks they have to pick their soulmate, but one woman's pretty much like the next. And Bridget, you want to stay away from her."

"I'm sorry, buddy, but I think Ralph is right. Love or no love, Bridget's bad news. Not Bridget, she's a nice girl, but if you want to live a nice long life and celebrate your golden anniversary, you need to find another girl, because she's already gone through two men, and she's likely to go through five or six more before she hits that golden anniversary stage."

Shawn reached up and pulled the cape from around his neck. A bunch of hair fell to his shoulder before Drake realized what he was doing and pulled his hands away.

"Hey! Wait. I'm not done."

"I know. But I am." He reached into his back pocket and pulled out his wallet. "I can pay for half a haircut, or I can pay for the whole thing. But I'm leaving."

"Well, I've never actually charged anyone for half a haircut, but I guess that's fair," Drake muttered to himself as he set his instruments down, brushed his hands off, then walked to the cash register.

"You don't need to get so huffy," Philip said.

"We're just trying to protect you," Ralph added.

"I don't need protection from my fiancée. She's a beautiful woman, smart and generous and considerate. This town is being nothing but terrible to her. I'm sick of hearing it. I'm not going to stand for it. If you guys want to talk about it, that's fine. But I won't be here."

"Where are you going? I'm the only barbershop in town."

"Going out to the farm."

Drake stared at his head, and Shawn figured he knew what he was looking at. He'd only gotten one side of his head done. He hadn't had a haircut since July, and it was probably pretty obvious.

Nothing a ballcap wouldn't cover.

Drake gave him a price, and Shawn paid cash.

Even as he was walking out the door, his father's voice rang in his head, saying, "Take care of that lie now, son, or it's going to get too big for you to handle."

But for some reason, he ignored it.

Maybe it was the anger in his chest. He hadn't even really realized that that was what that burning, tight feeling was. Anger.

These men with their casual words didn't intend to be as mean as they were, he was sure, but he could see Bridget's moss-green eyes and the hurt in them.

He could see the cares, the worry, and the hardships she faced. The trials and the loss combined with the hardworking farm girl she had to be. She was shouldering it all.

Instead of the town rallying around her—which to be fair, maybe they had. Maybe they'd given her monetary help. Maybe they'd shown up for the funeral and given food. But this...This talk of the curse and warning strangers away. This was not helping. This was adding to her load and making her life harder.

And maybe his lie would make it even worse.

He'd claimed she was his fiancée.

First of all, she didn't have a ring. He'd just seen her bare finger.

Second of all, he had no plans to get married to her, and she probably had even less to get married to him. So, there had to be a breakup.

At that point, instead of helping her, he would just be hurting her. Because he could hear the whole town saying, oh yeah, that young man finally came to his senses and ditched Bridget because of the curse.

Yeah. He could hear that.

He stood on the sidewalk, his teeth gritted together, his hands fisted at his sides.

He felt helpless. What could he do to undo what he'd done and actually do what he had wanted to do which was defend her and get the town to see how terrible they were being, or better yet, get them to change?

He blew out a breath.

This seemed like a good time to call his dad.

His dad would tell him to get his butt right back in that barbershop and fix the lie before it got any bigger.

Maybe he'd better get in his car and drive away before he made that call.

It turned out he never did make the phone call. By the time he'd stopped at the carwash and swept out his truck and then opened an account at the local bank, it was more than an hour, and he figured that Bridget might be waiting on him. So he drove straight out to the farm.

He might be 30 and had been on his own for more than a decade, but he really did crave his dad's advice and opinion.

More than that, though, he wondered exactly how much of this his dad already knew before he sent Shawn out. It was definitely going to be an interesting phone call.

But first, he needed to admit what he'd done to Bridget. Let her know that the town thought they were engaged.

He laughed a little, sure that if he were actually going to pop The Question to a woman, he couldn't be more nervous than what he was right now.

At least he already knew her answer.

He just wasn't sure how she was going to react to finding out that she'd said yes.

Chapter 5

B ridget pulled her SUV into the dirt parking spot beside the farmhouse just as a bolt of lightning split the air, branching off into countless shoots and tentacles slashing through the gloomy darkness that had descended, flashing with brilliance before disappearing into expectant silence before the crack and boom of thunder crashed around them.

"Are we going to get a tornado?" Portia asked softly, her voice trembling a little.

"I'll check the weather," Bridget said immediately, pulling her phone out.

She was grateful there were no other cars aside from the beat-up, old farm truck parked over by the barn.

Shawn must have gotten distracted with something else and hadn't made it to the farm yet.

Or maybe he'd been more disturbed about her talk about the curse than he'd let on, or upon further reflection, he'd decided he valued his life too much to do a favor for his dad that would most likely get him killed.

She felt relief.

Perhaps if she told herself that often enough, she'd actually start to feel relief instead of this sinking, biting feeling that felt a lot like disappointment.

She'd been disappointed in her life. Lots of times. But she was far more experienced with grief and sadness and loneliness and being overwhelmed-with-responsibility-ness, if that was a thing, and disappointment hadn't been something she allowed herself to feel too much.

You took what you got, and you moved on with it.

Except, it kept getting harder and harder with each blow, and at this point, she felt more like giving up than she did like digging in and fighting.

"There aren't any warnings. It looks like we're just going to get some much-needed rain."

Typically, they didn't get much severe weather in the fall, but Portia, at eight years old, was old enough to understand that Iowa weather didn't always do what it was supposed to do.

Not to mention she'd lived through enough springs where they'd run to the storm cellar both during the day and in the middle of the night that she had a healthy fear and a deep respect for tornadoes.

On a clear day with no wind, they could hear the tornado siren in town.

On a stormy day, with the wind blowing the way it was now? Probably not.

It definitely wouldn't wake them up, and it probably wouldn't penetrate the walls of the house even if they were awake.

"Okay, girls, looks like it could start raining anytime, so I need you to carry your school stuff in and then come back out and grab the groceries. Maybe we can get them all in before we get wet."

"Yes, ma'am," Robin and Elyse said together.

"What about the lightning?" Portia asked, still sounding scared.

"I don't think it's close enough that we have to worry about it right now. Not if we hurry."

If anything ever happened, she'd spend the rest of her life kicking herself that it had been more important to get the groceries in and out of the rain than keeping her kids protected from lightning. But in her experience, they would be fine.

There was that fine line between being safe and being reasonable, in living a life that didn't allow fear to control it.

She supposed everyone had to find their own line.

As she'd gotten older, her line had grown closer and closer to the fear instead of the reasonable.

She supposed there weren't too many people that would blame her.

As soon as she pulled the latch on her door, her girls followed. Elyse struggled some, because she'd brought her French horn home to practice, and it was almost as big as she was. She was small and fine-boned like her father had been.

Bridget probably shouldn't have married him. He'd moved to Iowa with his parents when he was a teenager and had come from out east.

There wasn't anything wrong with easterners, they just weren't tough and strong like a person needed to be in order to love the wide-open spaces of Iowa, to love her despite the weather, the storms, the wind, the freezing subzero temperatures, and the yearly blizzards. It was a harsh climate but a beautiful land. Still, it took a certain amount of fortitude and toughness to settle in and love it, thrive in it.

Patrick hadn't had that.

She grabbed as many bags as she could out of the back of the car, thinking again of Shawn and how he'd dealt with the cart, then sat and ate a watermelon.

Shawn was definitely the kind of man who would not just survive but thrive in Iowa.

He was tough but not a hothead daredevil the way Blade, her second husband, had been.

She'd gone from one extreme to the other.

Putting her head down against the wind, she speed-walked into the house, using one finger and a thumb to turn the doorknob, grateful to Robin who caught the door before it blew against the wall as she stepped in.

"Thank you," she said breathlessly as Robin walked out and closed the door behind her. She set the bags on the table and turned, opening the door to run back out and get another load.

She stopped short as the door widened and a man stepped into the kitchen.

Shawn.

He was a little out of breath, and he blew in just as the rain started pounding on the roof, and Robin and Elyse ran the last two steps up to the porch.

"That man got everything, and all I had to do was shut the trunk." Robin ran onto the porch, eyeing the tall cowboy who seemed to fill up the kitchen.

"That's fine. Come on in." Bridget opened the door wider, and everyone tramped into the kitchen.

She hadn't told the girls about Shawn. Maybe part of her thought that she would jinx the idea that someone was actually coming to help if she talked about it. Or counted on it. Part of her thought she'd scared him away with her talk of the curse.

But no jinx; he stood in her kitchen.

Although there was something odd about him.

Leaning back against the door, she narrowed her eyes, and when he turned, she said, "I hope you didn't pay full price for that haircut."

He laughed.

Then his laugh ended in kind of a nervous grunt, and he ran one hand over the top of his head, catching the longer strands. His cheeks seemed to redden under his tan.

"Well. I did. But there's a story behind it. And I have a confession to make, and something that we'll probably need to talk about and make a decision about."

"We?"

He nodded and then looked around. "These must be the girls you were talking about."

"Yes. My daughters. This is Robin, she's twelve."

She pointed to her eldest daughter, with her long, dark, almost black hair and dark eyes.

Robin smiled at Shawn, but her smile was guarded. She was old enough to be suspicious of people. She was also old enough to hear the townspeople saying that her mother was cursed.

Bridget hated what that did to her, but she didn't know what to do about it. Short of selling the farm and moving, and that was her last option. The last thing she wanted to consider.

"And this is Elyse. She's eleven."

Robin had only been three months old when she'd gotten pregnant with Elyse. Elyse had never met her father, who had died before she was born. She didn't look quite as much like her dad as Robin did.

Her hair was slightly lighter, and her eyes more hazel than brown. She walked around with her head in the clouds all the time, daydreaming as well. But she was so obedient and willing to please, with such a sweet personality, if not somewhat shy.

Probably her shyness was enabled by Robin who was outgoing and afraid of nothing. And if Elyse didn't feel like talking, she didn't have to because Robin would do it for her.

"And this is Portia. She's eight." Portia looked exactly like her father, Blade, with curly, blond hair and blue eyes, although she had Bridget's slender frame and not the tough bulkiness of her dad. Maybe she was a little spoiled being the last, and she was definitely the worrier.

"Girls, this is Shawn. He's thinking about helping us for a while."

"I'm going to help you for a while," Shawn corrected her, giving her a level glance, before his face broke into a smile as he looked at each of the girls. "It's good to meet you girls. Glad to see your mom has such good help."

Elyse just smiled, nodding.

Robin said, "You're going to live here?"

"I'm not sure," Shawn replied, truly sounding unsure.

"Your hair looks funny," Portia said with the forthrightness of an eight-year-old.

"It's not polite to tell people they look funny," Bridget said, realizing she already had.

Normally, she didn't correct her children in front of people, but if Shawn was going to be a part of the family, she might as well treat him that way.

No. Not a part of the family. Someone who worked here.

"I don't really have any place for you to stay other than the house," she said slowly.

"I see. Well...I need to talk to you anyway. I really hadn't given a thought about where I was going to stay. I hadn't realized I was going to be here alone with a woman and her children. I had assumed the friend was a man, and you know the rest."

"I do."

It was obvious he was uncomfortable and didn't want to stay alone with her. She had to admit that eased her mind almost more than anything he had done. It told her he was the kind of man who had morals. Standards. And he didn't go around doing whatever was convenient and felt right to him.

A little of the tightness in her chest eased, and she hadn't even realized it had been balled up.

She'd already thought Shawn was a good man. If he was a moral man as well, she probably should try even harder to talk him out of staying.

She'd managed to get married twice to men she liked but didn't love. Ones who liked her and loved that she came with a farm they would inherit and that would be worth something someday.

She was fine trading on that. As long as they were kind to her, she didn't need or want a huge love affair. She just wanted stability and a good life. A place to raise her children and a man to stand beside her.

Attraction and passion and all of those things were frivolous. Stuff she could live without.

Lightning flashed. Thunder cracked right behind it. Then the lights went out.

It wasn't pitch dark or anything, since it was late afternoon, although even without the cloud cover, dusk would be falling soon.

"Mom?" Portia said, her voice holding a thread of fear.

"It's okay, Portia. I'm here." Elyse walked to her sister and put her arm around her.

"Do you have a generator?" Shawn's voice startled her, low and deep. It wasn't necessarily even the rough maleness of his voice, even though that was unusual in their house, but it was the idea that there was another adult to help her in this minor emergency.

"No. No generator other than the one that runs the chicken house. I'd better look and make sure the lights are on there."

"I can do it. Is it that long building that was setting to the south?"

"Yes. You should be able to just stand on the porch and look. I believe the curtains were down. They should have been since it's so warm out."

"Got it." While he stepped outside, she went to the pantry and grabbed a couple of candles, then walked to the kitchen drawer and pulled out the matches.

By the time he'd stepped back in, she had two candles lit. They didn't necessarily need them, but it gave a cozier glow to the kitchen. "Looks like you girls get to do your schoolwork by candlelight," she said, trying to sound cheerful.

"Are we going to go up and do the eggs?" Robin asked.

"Maybe that would be a good thing for Mr. Shawn and me to do. I need to show him around the farm anyway."

"Okay. I have a lot of homework today," Robin said, moving toward her backpack which she'd set on the floor against the wall.

Normally when she brought the kids home from school, they changed their clothes and went directly to the chicken house to finish them up for the night. Once they were done with the barn work, the girls did their homework at the table while she cooked supper. Any of the girls who didn't have homework helped her.

Sometimes in the winter, she let the girls play after they did the chickens, and they did their homework in the evening after supper.

Regardless, the chickens always needed to be done, and while the work wasn't hard, strenuous, or labor intensive, what made it tough was that it needed to be done every day, seven days a week, three hundred sixty-five days a year.

That was farming.

Shawn hadn't said anything, so she asked, "Would that be okay with you?"

"Sure." He glanced around the table with the girls who were sitting down and getting their schoolwork out. "Unless you usually do it as a family. I don't want to interrupt."

"You're not. You can see they're not exactly heartbroken that they're not going to have to do the chickens today."

"Well, just as long as they don't think this is gonna be a thing," Shawn said, and there was humor in his tone, which made her grin. They hadn't talked about his past; all their conversation had been about her.

The way he related to her girls made her wonder if maybe he had children of his own. Maybe he was naturally good with kids.

Not that she cared. He wasn't staying. Obviously, that was going to be something that she was going to forget and needed to keep reminding herself.

"If you hang on a second, I'd like to go change my clothes."

She wouldn't get that dirty while they did the chickens, but she did like to keep the clothes she wore to the barn separate from the ones she didn't.

Chapter 6

I t took her a little longer than normal, because the house was dark. But she was back downstairs as quickly as she could be and walked into the kitchen where Shawn and the girls were talking about cattle.

Had one of them told him about their little Jersey cow? Buttercup. Portia had named her when she was three.

Shawn was talking about an Ayrshire herd that one of his buddies owned back in Arkansas, and he talked with such feeling in his voice that she had no doubt he loved his state.

It reminded her again that she was just a favor he was doing.

Cautioning herself to be grateful and not annoyed that she was an inconvenience, she waited until he was done with the story, and the girls were giggling, and she was smiling, before she said, "Are you ready?"

"Sure. Although, the girls said Buttercup has horns. Is it possible I'm going to be attacked by a cow between here and the chicken house?"

"As long as you scratch her right behind the crown of her head, Buttercup will do anything you want."

"The girls said she was tame, but..." He glanced over at them, humor in his eyes and wearing a mock concerned look. "But I wasn't sure whether they were saying that just to get my guard down, and she's actually a killer cow, and they'll all be standing at the window watching her charge me and giggling behind their hands."

Robin smiled, Elyse giggled, and Portia outright laughed.

Shawn opened the door, and Bridget stepped out.

"Looks like you won their hearts. That didn't take long," she said as she waited on the porch while he closed the door and stepped beside her.

"They're good girls. Sweet." He seemed to stumble a little over his words as they started off the steps together and down the well-worn path toward the chicken barn, with Bridget going in the lead and Shawn falling into step behind her.

"I...I know that with my sisters and my sisters-in-law that the best way to butter them up is to go through their children."

"That would make sense. But I can't see any reason for you to be buttering me up. It looked to me like you're being nice to them just because."

"That's true. I have to admit I do have a confession to make."

His tone made her stop and turn, but she caught herself before she moved the whole way around. The girls could see them from the window, and although they were probably doing their homework, she didn't want them to glance up and see the two of them stopped on the path halfway between the chicken barn and think there was a problem.

"You're concerning me," she said as she started off again, her steps not nearly as brisk.

What kind of bombshell was he going to drop? Had he decided already that he was leaving? She almost grunted. It would have been easier for him to just not show up. Easier for her than for him to come, make them all see what they would be missing, just to tell her that he wasn't going to stay.

She would have preferred him to just fade away quietly rather than give her hope.

"I think you're going to be concerned. I did something that I probably shouldn't have. And...I can't see any way out of it."

"Okay. Did you get in trouble in town?" She knew the sheriff. He was over the whole county and not just Prairie Rose. But it was unlikely that Shawn would have gotten in trouble, arrested, and bailed himself out of jail that quickly.

"I didn't get a call from the jail, so I assume it wasn't that kind of trouble," she finally said.

They'd reached the chicken barn, but instead of going to the door, she went to the end where Buttercup had sought protection from the storm.

"Here's our Jersey, and as you can see, she's a sweetie pie," Bridget said, scratching Buttercup behind the crown of her head where she loved it and then scratching her neck. The cow was wet from the rain that had poured for five minutes then stopped but was used to being out in the elements and was fine.

"I can't believe you just let her run around."

"We pen her up in the winter. There's no reason for her to run around then, and we need to have her where we can water and feed and milk her."

"You're not milking her now? The girls didn't mention it."

"No. She's dry. We're expecting a baby around Christmas, and we're giving her a few months off."

"I see. That probably makes it easier for you, too. One less chore you have to worry about."

"Exactly. Although, there's just something really soothing about milking a cow. Well, actually, it depends on the cow. Buttercup's a sweetheart, but the Jersey we had before her hated being milked. That wasn't quite as nice."

"I see. I imagine that might take some of the relaxation out of going out to milk."

"Yeah. When you're fighting for your life, it's kind of hard to live in the moment and enjoy it."

"Right. So... I'm gonna take it that cow didn't die of old age?"

His question made her smile. She loved that he got the whole farming thing, which was something she hadn't shared with either one of her previous husbands.

"You're taking it right. She fed us all winter about four winters ago. And I savored every bite."

She took a glance at him to see him smiling, and she laughed outright. Not everyone would enjoy her morbid humor, but she loved that he got it. She supposed every profession shared that. Accountants had their own workplace humor. If accountants had humor, which Bridget supposed was debatable. So did office workers and mechanics. They all had things that they could laugh about with insider knowledge.

Farming was the same way, only it was slightly harsher, closer to death, closer to the things that could make people sensitive and upset. She wasn't going to have to worry about tiptoeing around Shawn's feelings or delicate sensibilities.

That was a relief.

Not that he was staying, she reminded herself yet again.

He hadn't even been here a day, and she could already see him long-term.

"What was this terrible thing that you've done that you need to confess?" she asked as he ran a hand down Buttercup's neck. The cow lifted her head so he could scratch under her jaw.

"I went into the barbershop to get a haircut."

"Yeah, and you got cheated on that," Bridget interrupted him.

"About that, well, maybe we should back up even further," Shawn said.

Bridget lifted her brows but didn't say anything as he scratched the sweet spot at Buttercup's throat, and Bridget gave her brisket a good rub.

"You'd mentioned about this curse thing, which I'm not buying into, not at all. Not even a little bit, and it kinda made me mad."

"I'm sorry. I didn't mean to make you mad," Bridget said quickly, wondering if she was the one who had scared him away, then remembering that had been her intention.

She gave herself a mental kick.

She kinda liked him.

That wasn't true.

She really liked him.

He was kind, easygoing, got along with the girls...at least so far, and he knew where to scratch a cow.

She didn't need to know anything else since all that made him pretty much perfect.

"Anyway, I was already a little stirred up, and when I went in to get my haircut, of course they wanted to know what I was doing in town."

"Small towns, right?"

"Exactly. So, like I hadn't grown up in a small town, I told him what I was here for and mentioned you."

"Now I know what happened."

"Yeah. The curse."

"And they told you how you need to stay away from me. How everyone around me dies, and you shouldn't even set foot on the farm, definitely shouldn't stay here, and shouldn't have anything to do with me, even if I do move off the farm."

Bridget said everything slowly, evenly, and tried to keep the emotion out of her voice. The townspeople meant well. They loved her. She knew they did, they just thought there was a problem with her and felt like it was their job to let everyone who came to town know about it.

"You got it."

"That's fine. I'm not upset that you changed your mind. They could be right. I mean they are right. I told you that they were."

She swallowed hard and bent over, focusing on Buttercup's brisket, scratching up and down both sides, knowing that Buttercup just loved it.

"You don't have to stay. There's no point in you even being here one night. No one needs to be told anything. You were doing a favor; it didn't work out. And if you're worried about your dad or my dad or whatever, you don't need to be. There are no hard feelings here, and in fact, I would feel guilty if something did happen. You're saving my stress levels and doing me a favor by leaving."

She was rambling, trying to get all the words out, making sure that he understood that she didn't give a flip and was just as happy to see him walk away as she was to see him stay.

He cleared his throat. "Well...that's not exactly what happened."

His tone made her head flip up, and she narrowed her eyes, trying to figure out what in the world he could have done that would be worse than the townspeople saying that she was cursed and people from out of town should stay away.

"What happened?"

Shawn seemed to find Buttercup's brisket very interesting. "I told them we were engaged."

Her breath left her in a huff, and she stared, her hands still, the cow forgotten.

"You what?" she asked, sure she must have heard him wrong. "I thought you said you told him we were engaged." And then she laughed. That was funny. Right?

"Yeah, that's what I said."

"Like, marriage engaged?" Maybe that was a stupid question, but there were other types of engagement, right? They could be engaged in working or engaged as in busy.

"Yeah. Like the kind of engagement that leads to marriage. I didn't tell them a date. I left before they could ask me too many questions. Stormed out, maybe," he said, and she realized that he wasn't joking. He'd left before Drake had finished his haircut.

He was looking at her like he was afraid she was going to be upset.

Maybe she wasn't having the right kind of reaction, the kind of reaction a normal person would have, but she was trying not to laugh. Like rolling-on-the-floor laughter wanted to come out of her chest in great big gulps, but she pushed it down.

He definitely didn't look like he thought it was funny.

"I'm having a hard time not laughing about this," she finally admitted, kinda soft but with a little strain in her voice. A telltale sign that showed she really was trying to keep the laughter contained in her lungs and not bursting out her mouth.

"I don't understand what's funny." Shawn stopped petting the cow and stared at her.

"I'm not sure I can explain what is either, I just really feel like laughing." It was true. There wasn't a single thing that was funny about the situation, other than maybe irony. Since it was the exact opposite thing of whatever she'd expected him to do. "Did you tell them you were kidding?"

"No, that's just it. I don't usually lie. I can't remember the last time I said something that wasn't true. But I did, and I knew when the words were coming out of my mouth it was a lie, and I knew as soon as I said it, I should correct myself, say I was kidding, say it was a joke, say I haven't asked her yet even, something that was true, something to make the lie not a lie anymore, except...I didn't."

"So...you want *me* to tell everyone we're not engaged?" The laughter had faded out of her lungs, and a little bit of bitterness took its place. Of course. He didn't want to face up to his lie, but he certainly didn't want to be engaged to her. So he was giving her the job of correcting things in the town.

"No. Absolutely not. If I wanted to correct the lie, I'd do it myself. The thing is, even as I walked to my truck and drove out of town, I didn't want to correct it."

"Wait. You want the town to think we're engaged?" She tried not to sound shocked. "Why?"

Buttercup rolled her head as his hand found the sweet spot behind the crown. "Because. I was at the grocery store, barbershop, then I went to the bank. In every place I went, as soon as they found out what I was going to be doing, or as soon as they heard your name, the curse was in their eyes and out their mouth. I haven't even been in town for a full day, and I'm sick of it. It's gonna stop. I'm going to stop it."

"Those are big words. The curse has been going on for a while now. You rolling into town and telling everyone it's garbage is hardly going to fix it."

"I know that," he said. "But maybe me rolling into town, and saying I'm engaged to you, and not dying, might."

She quit petting Buttercup and straightened, crossing her arms over her chest, like she needed that protection. "You're serious. You actually said that. That we're engaged."

"Yeah." His word was firm, and he looked down, straightening, shoving his hands in his pockets.

Buttercup, annoyed that both of her admirers had quit petting her, pushed her head against Shawn's hip, reminding him that as long as she was around, he had a job to perform.

One hand came out of his pocket, and he absently scratched her face.

"I'm sorry. I actually was laughing a little, because on the way here, I was extremely nervous about having to tell you." One corner of his mouth ticked up, and her heart did a little sideways step at the cuteness of his smile. "I've never actually asked anyone to marry me, but probably the nervousness that I was feeling is about the way a guy would feel, only I already put the yes in your mouth, I just had to tell you about it."

His eyes were twinkling, and even though he'd done something that she wasn't sure how she was going to fix, she had to laugh, too.

"I hope you were eaten up with anxiety." She shook her head, chuckling. "I don't know how I'm going to fix this." She slapped a hand against her leg and started toward the chicken barn door. "Actually, I think it may be worse. Because when you leave, they'll automatically assume we broke up, and they'll also assume that the curse scared you away."

"I had considered that."

"But I guess that's no worse than what it is right now. I mean come on, no matter what we say, when you leave, they're going to assume the curse scared you. Whether we were engaged or whether we're not. It's not going to hurt anything. But"—she shifted to the side as he stepped forward and took the door from her, indicating for her to go first—"it's not going to help anything either."

"It could."

"I'm sorry, but I don't see how," she said, walking through and waiting for him to come in as well.

"I do."

"Okay. I guess you can let me know, because I'm just not seeing it." She didn't really think he was going to come up with anything. She was positive she hadn't missed anything.

It wouldn't matter, no matter how deeply in love they pretended to be, how safe he was. Even if nothing ever happened to him, as soon as he left, everyone would say it was because of the curse. They would twist it around somehow.

"I'm going to stay," Shawn said, simply and matter-of-factly. Like he'd already decided. When he had told her quite clearly not three hours ago that he wasn't going to stay.

She stepped on the antibacterial mat and indicated for him to do the same before she walked over to change into her barn shoes. "I suppose it might work, but if you're gonna stay, I'm going to assume you're gonna buy a house somewhere, and you won't actually be living on the farm. That won't exactly help."

"That's true. But...there is one thing that would."

"Would what?"

"Would help."

"What's that?"

"I'll stay, and you'll marry me."

Chapter 7

Shawn couldn't quite believe what he'd just done.

His dad always warned him you need to catch a lie before it becomes too big for you to contain.

He held his breath, because if Bridget agreed with the crazy idea that had just come out of his mouth, the lie would officially be too big for him to contain.

But he couldn't find it in himself to regret the lie or the words he'd just said.

"You're suggesting a real marriage?"

"A marriage of convenience maybe," he said easily. At least his words came out easily. Inside, his chest was doing all kinds of writhing and wouldn't settle down. He had a feeling the nervousness threatening to take over his heart and lungs was not concerned that the lady was going to say yes. It was concerned that she was going to turn him down.

Why did he care so much?

If he were truly just doing a favor, a favor that had turned into a lie that had turned into more, why was he so invested in this?

He'd only just met her this afternoon. Lunchtime.

That phone call to his dad might be a little more complicated than he'd originally anticipated.

"Oh." Something flashed across Bridget's eyes before she turned away. He had a feeling he could have handled that a little better. "It's nothing that's going to last?" She walked over to a large table at the end of what he assumed must be the egg belt. He wasn't exactly familiar with chicken houses, although he'd seen a few online. He'd deliberately looked them up when he realized he was coming to Iowa for a while.

"I meant a real marriage. Just not a traditional courtship. Something where we look at our circumstances and decide that the best thing for both of us would be to get married. Because it solves some of your problems and mine."

"You have problems?" she asked, then immediately her expression changed, and she said, "I'm sorry. Everyone has problems. I didn't mean it like that."

"No. I understand. I guess you're wondering what I would get out of a marriage of convenience."

"Yeah. That's right. Since all we've been talking about is me. My problems. You're familiar with them."

"Yeah. The curse. But also, you need someone to help you here on the farm."

"You would be a good father to the girls as well?" It almost came out as a statement, but there was a little lift at the end, indicating while she thought he might be a good father, she was asking if that was part of his plan.

Like he had a plan.

"Of course. A good husband, hopefully. A good father. I'd have to work on it all. I've never had any experience."

"I've been a mother and a wife, and I swore I would never be a wife again."

She let the statement dangle there, and he took three breaths before he said, "Is that something you're willing to reconsider?"

"Maybe. I suppose. I don't really care about the curse though. That's the way Prairie Rose has been for as long as I can remember. Used to be just the farm that they said was cursed. Now I get lumped into it. And in order to leave the curse behind, I have to completely move out of the area. I don't want to do that. So I've just learned to live with it."

"I noticed. But it bothers me."

"Maybe you'll get used to it too."

"Or maybe we'll get them to change their minds."

"Marriage seems like a pretty drastic step."

"I'll be honest. It was a step I wasn't considering. Had never considered with anyone. Normally when I make decisions that affect the rest of my life, I take a little time to think about them. Pray about them. Talk to some trusted counselors. But the lie is out there, and we can make it truth. And I'm okay with that."

"You don't even know me."

"I know your father was a friend of my father's. I know my dad thought a lot of him. I know if my dad had any questions or concerns about you, he would have told me about them. I'm sure, over the years, your dad has talked to him about you. Actually, my parents are known somewhat as matchmakers, and it wouldn't surprise me to find out they sent me out here with that in mind."

"I would think you'd be running in the other direction. That's the way most people respond to their parents' attempted matchmaking."

"You don't know my parents. They're good. And I trust them. I couldn't get wiser counsel from anyone."

"I see." A look that he almost considered admiration passed across her face. He thought maybe she liked the fact that he admired and respected his parents. It wasn't a typical thing for an adult to be doing.

"I guess we can just leave the offer on the table if you feel like you need some time to think about it. I understand that marriage is a big step and not something entered into lightly. But I also think that you and I can be friends. Good friends. And I've seen a lot of people start out with a lot less and a lot worse foundation."

"I agree with that. I've done it twice."

She didn't add anything to that, and he was left to wonder about it.

But she didn't give him time to comment. "I don't need time to think about it. If that's what you want to do, I'm down for it, too."

He couldn't help it; both of his lips curved up. Maybe he was crazy. Of all his siblings, he was the one who was known for being a little nutty. For taking risks and being the goofball of the family.

Wasn't marriage always a risk?

People who had known each other for years before marrying still got divorced.

Even people who had dated, people who lived together, people who felt like they knew their potential spouse inside and out, even those people got divorced.

It was all about sticking.

From what he'd heard about Bridget today, she wasn't a quitter. She'd stay. She wasn't going to get tired and give up. If she made vows, lifetime vows, she'd keep them.

He wasn't quite sure what had convinced her to take him, but something had, and he wasn't going to be changing his mind either. Once he made a commitment, he'd see it through.

The only thing that gave him a little bit of a pause was the tug his family and hometown had on his heart. The idea of leaving them forever and starting a new life hundreds of miles away pulled the corners of his mouth down and twisted his chest just a little.

"Change your mind already?" she asked with a glance at him before she went to a small room in the corner of the packing room they were standing in.

He followed her. "No. I was just thinking, wondering really, what made you decide to say yes."

"I guess I could ask you the same question," she said, stopping in front of a large box on the wall and looking at him over her shoulder.

"I can see you're not a quitter. I can see you won't back down. I can see it doesn't matter what people say, you can continue to walk ahead and do right, and you'll do it alone if necessary. That's all I need to know to be confident I'll be getting a wife who will be faithful and will still be beside me fifty years from now."

His words must have pleased her, because her eyes smiled even if her lips didn't.

"And you?" he asked. Yeah, maybe he was fishing for a compliment.

"You're the best offer I've had today. I might as well take you up on it."

Not exactly what he was looking for. But he supposed it served him right.

Still, it irked a little.

Couldn't she think of one good thing to say about him? She must have thought there was something good with him, since she'd agreed to turn his lie into truth.

"This is our computer system. It pretty much has all our information and controls everything. It tells us how much feed the birds eat, how much water they drink, it's how we set the lights to go on and off, and it controls the fans in the barn and the curtains as well."

"The curtains are automatic?"

"Everything is automatic. We updated about three years ago and haven't had any problems other than a couple of snapped chains on the feeders and one burnt-out motor on the curtains."

"Nice."

"Yeah. But it can make you complacent. Every day, we need to check everything. Make sure it's all working. Even a few hours, in ninety-five-degree heat, if the curtains aren't working, or the fans don't come on, we can lose a lot of birds. You have to stay on it."

"I see."

"Also, if the feeders don't work, or for some reason the feed's not coming out of the bins, and the birds are without feed for a day, production's gonna drop. You might never get it back."

"I get that."

She went on, talking about the things they had to watch for, and he was impressed because she really knew her stuff. She should though, since the chicken house was supporting the farm as far as he knew.

She probably rented her fields out, although he didn't know for sure. But normally, that did nothing more than cover taxes. Although even having taxes covered was a good thing.

They left the little room, and she went over to the sink where a blue wire basket sat on the counter.

"When the girls and I are here, I usually go out and walk around and pick up the floor eggs, and the girls start the belt. You can come out with me, although the chickens aren't used to you and you're going to scare them. So walk slowly, and try not to make any big movements."

"Okay. Is this gonna be something I shouldn't do?"

"No. They're gonna have to get used to you at some point. They'll recognize that you're not a regular, and it will take a week or so until you can walk around almost normally." She gave a little smile.

"Almost normally?"

"I always take it slow in there. It's not good for them to run, and, as you will see, when a couple of them start running, eventually the entire barn is running, and then you have a chicken stampede."

"That's new." He grinned.

She returned it. "I know. You don't hear about it, because it's not like a cattle stampede, where people get killed. But the chickens can kill themselves, because they make it to the end of the barn and just pile up on each other. Obviously, we don't want that to happen."

"No. I see. Every chicken that dies is money out of your pocket."

"Exactly. Also, 'a righteous man regardeth the life of his beast.' It's our job to take care of them."

"I like that verse."

"Me too. It gives a standard that no government or humane agency can hold a candle to. I don't answer to them. I answer to the Lord."

"You guys are certified humane?"

"Yes."

"Organic?"

"No. I've considered it, because it is more money. But it's just too expensive to feed them and eats into more of your profits than it's worth."

"I see."

She opened the door, and they walked out. Bridget had been right. The chickens scattered in front of him.

Maybe it was because she was walking first, or maybe he just wasn't used to it, but she was bending over and picking up eggs before he even saw them on the ground. By the time they'd made it the whole way around, the big basket was full.

He waited to talk until they'd gotten out of the barn area and back into the packing room. The chickens were just too loud to be heard without shouting.

"That's a lot of eggs. Do you get any on the belt?" He nodded at the basket that she carried. Belatedly, he realized he should have offered to carry it. It looked heavy.

She laughed. "This is nothing compared to what you're going to see. Although the heaviest amount of eggs is in the morning, of course."

"Of course." Like he knew. "How many eggs are in the basket?"

"Probably not quite two hundred."

"That seems like a lot."

"It is. This flock has been pretty bad for laying floor eggs." She lifted a shoulder and set the basket on the counter carefully. "Every flock is different. They have their own personality. They're really kind of a unit, although you do have individual outliers. But the flock seems to become almost a living entity of its own, if that makes sense."

"You mean the chickens kind of follow each other, and they all start doing the same thing?"

"Basically, I guess. It's weird, some flocks lay early in the morning, some flocks lay late, and some flocks lay eggs all day long. And that's just one thing. Some flocks are scary, some flocks are pretty calm." She turned the water on and set the basket down in the deep sink. "It also depends on what type of bird you get. Some breeds are known for being flighty, and others are known for being too lazy to get off the floor to lay their eggs in the nests."

He liked that she knew her stuff. He supposed she had to, considering she'd run the farm by herself since her dad died. They talked a little more about floor eggs and washing them, and she talked about the protective film that was on the egg and why they kept the eggs that had been washed separate from the ones that hadn't been.

Finally, as they were putting the last egg in the flat, she turned to him and said, "I feel like I need to tell you that the farm is mortgaged. Just in case you were thinking that you're getting a farm when you get me."

Her words weren't overly emotional. In fact, he would say they were delivered in the same tone she'd been talking about the eggs. It was the expression on her face that gave him pause.

He wanted to make sure he said this right, so he met her eyes steadily and let several moments pass before he spoke. "I'm guessing that one or both of your husbands married you for the farm."

Chapter 8

Bridget's lips twitched, and she looked away, busying her hands by wiping the sink and putting the basket on the floor.

Shawn figured he wasn't going to get an answer to that question.

She probably didn't need to answer it, because he could tell from the way she was avoiding looking at him that the answer was yes, obviously.

"I had a farm of my own in Arkansas. I think I told you that. It was close to being paid off, and in the ten years that I had it, property values in the area had really gone up. I made a substantial amount of money when I sold it."

She hadn't lifted her head, but she didn't move away, either.

"Even after taxes, I have more than enough to pretty much buy whatever I want. And I'm not saying that to brag, I'm saying that because I want you to understand that while I love the farm that you're on and what I've seen so far, I'm bringing value of my own to the table, which I know you're not marrying me for, since you didn't know about it?" He ended that statement like a question because he didn't know what she'd talked to his dad about. Maybe she did know that he came with money.

"I didn't know it, if that's what you're implying."

"I wasn't implying anything. I was asking. I guess I was just realizing that you probably talked to my dad, and I don't know what you two talked about."

"I didn't talk much. My dad and yours were the ones that had most of the conversations. Your dad came out for the funeral." She paused there.

He nodded, but he hadn't known. While he would say he had a great relationship with his dad, they didn't tell each other everything. He certainly hadn't realized his dad'd had a friend in Iowa and had been out for the funeral.

"I didn't know."

"I talked to him some then, and you must have been in the process of selling your farm, because he told me he had someone who knew farming and might be willing to come out. But that was earlier this spring, and you never showed up."

"I sold it, but we didn't close until after the crops were off."

"I see." She shut the water off and wrung out the rag, putting some water and Clorox in a bucket and then setting the rag in that. "Normally, I would do this job while the girls pick eggs off the belt. Let me show you how to do that."

"I've seen videos, but I've never actually been this close to it for real."

"I love it. I know that's cheesy, but this is my favorite part of everything that I do. It's just so much fun to see the eggs come out. I know it's little-kid crazy, but I love watching them."

"I can see how sometimes you get tired of stuff when you do it every day, but I think sometimes we get jaded or take things for granted when we shouldn't. Like sunsets."

"Or sunrises," she said with a smile.

"Some people aren't up early enough to appreciate the sunrise."

"When you have to get the eggs done before your kids go to school, it kind of forces you to get up a little earlier and get moving."

"I'll have to take your word on that. I haven't experienced that yet."

She put him on one side of the belt, and she stood on the other. She showed him how to run it, and he had to admit she was right. It was fun to watch the eggs come out, see the patterns, although after about three minutes, he dropped one.

"Oh, man. I didn't mean to do that."

She laughed. "We try not to, because obviously that cuts in the profits, but they're eggs. It's hard not to break one or two a day. Sometimes more."

"What do I do to clean it up?"

"We'll clean it up at the end. It probably won't be the only one you drop. Honestly, when you're just getting used to it, it takes a little while to get the knack."

"Hope I get it quickly, because it doesn't feel very good to drop them."

"Trust me, we've all done it."

They worked in silence for a little while, and he honestly was amazed at how quickly she went. Would he ever be that fast? Somehow, she just seemed more dexterous than he could ever imagine himself being.

But maybe he wouldn't be in here much. He'd assumed he'd be in the fields. Of course, with winter coming on, he might actually spend time here. They needed to talk about the equipment and if anything needed taking care of. He was pretty good at fixing things, although he needed the right tools, which she might not have.

Part of him wanted to get all of that settled and hashed out immediately, and part of him figured that it was probably best to take things slow.

So he didn't say anything more while they worked, and neither did she. In less than an hour, they were headed back to the house.

"That didn't take long."

"It takes about three times as long in the morning. There's a lot more eggs, both on the floor and on the belt. Sometimes, you have to make two or three trips with the basket."

"I guess we never figured out where I was going to stay."

If the question rattled her, she didn't show it. "The house has six bedrooms. There's only four of us. You have your choice of two." Her words were matter-of-fact. If she was thinking about where he might stay after they got married, he couldn't tell.

"Are you still good with actually going through with getting married?" he asked, feeling like it was a surreal thing.

"Of course. I said I was. I can't really see too many downsides. For me anyway. I've already been married twice, and I hardly think that the big love of my life is gonna show up and I'm going to be stuck with you and wish I wasn't." She glanced over her shoulder at him, and she was smiling a little, so he knew she didn't mean it as an insult. "But you might. Sure you don't want to hold out and wait for someone better to come along?"

"No." He was pretty sure no one better was going to come along. Funny how sure he was, considering how long he'd known her.

He would never claim it was a love match. Not in a million years, but he kinda thought he might grow to be affectionate with her, even if he didn't think he was going to fall in love with her. But at his age, he probably wasn't going to fall in love with anyone. He just wasn't that kind of man.

"How about we do this. I'll find a place to stay tonight, and I'll come out in the morning and do the barn work with you... What time do you usually do it?"

"We start by six. The girls help me for an hour or an hour and a half, then we quit, I take them to school, and then I come back and finish up myself."

"All right. I'll be here at six. You take the girls to school, and then I'll take you out for breakfast. We'll hash out the details of what we expect out of this marriage, and then we'll take care of it. If we can. If we can't, we'll at least get things started. After that, we'll come back here." He almost said home, but it felt too weird to be calling this farm home. "And you can show me around and let me know what all needs to be done, what I need to fix for the winter, to be ready for the spring, and we'll figure out where we're going to go from here. Sound good?"

He almost thought she was going to argue with him, because it took her a little while to answer. Then she said, "Yeah. Actually, that all sounds good."

"Really? You sure?" There had been some kind of hesitation in her tone, and he didn't want to push her.

"I guess I just wasn't planning on getting married tomorrow, but I'll get used to it, and tomorrow is as good a day as any."

They had made it to the house. Instead of turning toward the door, he said, "All right. I'll let you break it to the girls, and I'll be back in the morning."

"I'll see you in the morning," she said, giving him one last look that he couldn't read, before she turned and went in the house.

Chapter 9

Bridget stepped into the kitchen, realizing as she did so that the lights had come back on.

She hadn't even noticed while they'd been at the barn, since their generator was automatic and took care of everything. As it was supposed to do. Thankfully. She had no idea of what to do with the generator if it didn't work.

She didn't even know if that was something that Shawn would be able to take care of. At least she wouldn't be alone if she had to figure it out.

She'd barely shut the door behind her, and three sets of eyes had looked up from the table at her, when she realized two things.

The first was somehow, she had to figure out how to tell her children she was going to get married tomorrow. Wow. She hadn't even thought about that.

And that was the second thing. When was the last time she'd made a decision without weighing the pros and cons of the consequences to her children before she'd decided on a definite decision?

She couldn't remember the last time. Probably before she had children. She always considered them.

But this time...she hadn't.

Immediately though, she was fairly certain the pros would outweigh the cons.

But she made a mental note to ask Shawn for references tomorrow. It was definitely the least she could do to protect her kids.

She looked again at her girls, knowing instinctively that Shawn would be an excellent father. The problem was how was she going to justify a marriage of convenience for herself when she definitely didn't want her children to do such a thing.

She'd always tried to live by the principles that she wanted to model for her kids. She'd preached with her life and gave suggestions with her mouth. In her experience, especially with teenagers, lectures went in one ear and out the other. But kids watched what you did like a hawk.

She certainly had thought about her own mother that way over the years.

The pain her mother's leaving had inflicted, making her feel abandoned and unloved. Her mother's example had shown her what she absolutely did not want to do.

She didn't want to be the example of what not to do for her children.

Maybe she could just leave the marriage of convenience out.

Of course, Robin was old enough to know that a person didn't meet a man one day and marry him the next.

Bridget drew in a fortifying breath and smiled at her girls. "Did you all get your homework done?"

"Most of it. I have some math I need help with," Robin said.

"I need to finish reading this chapter, and then I'm done," Elyse said.

"I'm done. I wanted to start cooking supper, but Robin and Elyse wouldn't let me."

"That's because you burnt it the last time, and Mom had more work to do to try to scrape the stuff off the bottom of the pan, because you were crying that it was too hard." Robin wasn't speaking in the nicest voice.

"You're right, Robin. She did burn everything the last time. But you are not being very nice, and it's more important to be kind than right. So if you can't think of anything kind to say, don't say anything." She turned back to Portia. "It's probably best for you to have a little supervision before you try to make supper by yourself. Plus, if you had cooked it yourself, I wouldn't have the pleasure of cooking it with you. And I like cooking with you." Bridget smiled at her daughter, who beamed under her praise. "Let me wash my hands, and we'll get started on it."

Deciding that the best time to talk about her impending marriage on the morrow with Shawn would be at supper, she chatted with her girls about their school days and a field trip coming up, and one of the girls had a birthday as well. They were all laughing and having a good time by the time supper was ready to set on the table.

Bridget said the blessing, then she waited until the girls had had a chance to eat a little before she started.

"Mr. Shawn and I were talking while we were doing the eggs, and we decided to get married tomorrow."

That was about the worst way she could have broken it to them. But she wasn't exactly good at sugarcoating things. She didn't know how else to lead up to it.

Plus, when someone wanted to tell her something, she'd much rather they just come right out and tell her than beat around the bush.

Not surprisingly, her girls just stared at her.

"You're getting married?" Robin asked, confusion in her tone and on her face.

"I shouldn't have said it like that. I'm sorry. I know this is a little unexpected. And I also will beg off, even though I told him I would, if this is something that any of you are adamantly opposed to."

She would. She didn't like to go back on her word and in fact couldn't remember the last time that she had. But she would if even one of her girls had a major problem. She wouldn't destroy the relationship she had with her girls just for the convenience of having a man on the farm.

"I guess I don't really care. Although...is Shawn someone you've known for a while?" Robin still seemed to be trying to process the idea that their mother was getting married in the morning.

"No. But people that I trust, including your grandfather, think he is a good man."

She wasn't stretching the truth too much by saying that. Her dad wouldn't have allowed someone to come to the farm who he didn't think would be a good influence on his grandchildren or a good man for his daughter to be around, no matter how badly he needed the help.

"He's honest. He's not afraid to work, and we would be a family with a mom and a dad."

The girls all stared at her, none of them looking too upset but all of them as though they were thinking about it.

"I liked him. He was funny," Portia finally said.

She was the only one who actually had a dad that she remembered. Blade had been good with the older two girls, but they'd never called him anything other than Mr. Blade. Neither one of them had gotten comfortable enough with him to call him dad.

He wasn't exactly the lovey-dovey, cuddly type. And he didn't go out of his way to talk to them.

But he hadn't been abusive, and although he got angry, it wasn't typically at the girls.

He had dealt with them a couple of times, but it hadn't been a regular thing.

Shawn didn't seem like he had a temper, but maybe she wasn't reading him right.

"I liked him too. I guess if you have to get married, he's as good a guy as any. Isn't he afraid of the curse?" Elyse sounded very matter-of-fact, like she had grown up with the curse and knew it was a thing.

"He doesn't think there is a curse."

That's all she was going to say about that. She wasn't convinced there was a curse there, either. She figured it was more God being angry at her, but she hadn't taught that to her girls because she wanted them to love God, not resent Him because He was so mean to them.

In her heart of hearts, she knew it wasn't God being mean. But she did believe God was in control of everything, and sometimes she wondered why He let so many bad things happen to her. So many deaths. To the point where the town didn't exactly shun her but most certainly avoided her. Or at least had their menfolk avoid her.

She couldn't even hire anyone to help her.

Other than the Emerson brothers, her closest neighbors, but they were too busy with their own stuff to actually work full time. They helped when they could. Miss Matilda and they were pretty much the only people in town who hadn't gone all in about the curse.

"Doesn't he know about everybody who died?" Robin asked, and Bridget bit the inside of her lip. She hardly ever talked about the curse with her children. But obviously, they'd been hearing about it from somewhere else, since they all seemed to be acquainted with the details.

"He does. He thinks God is in charge and that what the Lord allows to happen, happens for a reason. And not because of some hocus-pocus curse thing." That's what she used to believe, too.

"Do you think he's right?" Elyse asked, sounding hopeful.

That hopeful tone cracked Bridget's heart. She thought the curse just pertained to her, but the girls obviously felt the shame of it as well. Even if they'd never said anything, and even if it didn't apply to them.

She hoped they didn't think it applied to them.

Chapter 10

Their conversation was interrupted by a quick knock at the door.

Bridget looked at it, rising slowly. Who in the world would be knocking on the door at this time in the evening?

It wasn't unheard of to get a visitor, but she wasn't expecting anyone.

Had Shawn come back for something? Her heart took a nosedive. For some reason, her hands went automatically to her hair, like it looked any different than it had when he'd left.

She'd just gotten to her feet when the door began to open.

She grunted, amused at herself. It was probably one of the Emerson brothers. They were her neighbors to the south and were like brothers to her.

Sure enough, after another second the door had opened wide enough for her to see Braxton standing in the doorway.

"Hello, the house?" he called out the traditional greeting before his eyes landed on the table where they sat.

"Come on in. You're just in time for supper."

"You know I won't turn down a home-cooked meal, except I just ate. And I don't think I could fit another bite in. But thanks."

"Oh? I thought that's why you showed up at suppertime?"

"Is that what time it is? It seems a little late."

She looked at the time, and sure enough, it was later than what she thought it was. The time had flown by while she and Shawn had been at the barn, and then she and the girls had been lingering over supper with the conversation that they'd been having.

"Mom's getting married," Portia offered before Bridget could say anything else.

"I heard that, Poppet," Braxton said, using the nickname he and his brothers all used for Portia. "That's actually why I'm here."

He smiled, but it didn't quite reach his eyes. She'd grown up with him, so it wasn't a problem to surmise that he was here because he was concerned about her.

Braxton and his brothers helped her as much as they could, and they were the ones who had rented her ground last year. But they were also busy in the different things that they were doing, trying to keep their own farm afloat along with all their other side businesses, that she hated to bother them for anything.

This probably wasn't a conversation she wanted to have in front of her girls, who weren't sure about the whole mommy getting married tomorrow thing anyway.

She didn't want Braxton, who didn't look very happy with her and the idea, turning their minds against it and forcing her to tell Shawn she'd changed her mind.

She walked away from the table, saying to her girls, "You can go ahead and say hi to Uncle Braxton, then you guys need to go upstairs and get your baths and get ready for bed. We'll play a game and read a few more chapters in our book once you guys are all ready."

"What about the dishes?" Elyse asked as she stood with her sisters.

"I'll take care of them." Bridget smiled at her daughter, appreciating her consideration.

The girls chatted with Braxton for just a few minutes, while Bridget worked at clearing the table off, before they scattered up the stairs, and she was left alone in the kitchen with a stern-looking almost-elder brother.

"What are you thinking, Bridget?"

"Really?" She paused with dirty dishes in her hand on the way to the sink. "Are you really gonna ask me that?"

"Do you know this dude?"

She didn't ask how he'd heard. It was a small town, after all. "My dad knew his father. And they both agreed for him to come. You know my dad would never have someone coming here that he didn't trust. Especially since he knew he wasn't going to be around long."

Her argument was rational, and Braxton's expression recognized that fact. Still, while the glower eased, it didn't disappear.

"If you want to have some dude here working full time, just talk to me. I can do more."

"And you would have to sacrifice sleep in order to do that. I won't have you killing yourself to work on my farm when your own farm needs you just as badly."

"I sleep too much anyway." His dark eyes had maybe a twinkle in them, even though his lips didn't turn up. Braxton always was the most serious of the brothers. Serious and driven and almost aloof.

It wasn't a shock to anyone when he left the farm out of high school and didn't come back for several years.

What had been a shock to the entire community, was several years after that when he took a trip, coming back with his six-year-old daughter who looked exactly like him.

No mother.

Braxton had confided to Bridget one summer day when they'd been making hay together that he had been deeply and passionately in love with his daughter's mother. And, in fact, still was.

For all intents and purposes, he'd hinted that the mother of his daughter loved him as well.

When Bridget had pressed and asked why they weren't together, she thought he'd said she was imprisoned.

But his brothers had taken that time to show up on the four-wheeler, and his words had been drowned out by the rumble of the motor, and she hadn't asked again.

As far as she knew, no one else knew anything about Arian's mother.

"All of my brothers would pitch in too. You know that."

She wrung out the dishrag she was going to use to wipe the table and put one hand on her hip. "I know that. I know you all would. But how would you feel if you had to rely on the generosity and charity of your neighbors in order to get your work done? You'd hate it." She answered her own question before he could open his mouth. "Just as I do. Having Shawn around will make it so that I don't have to constantly ask you for help every time a tractor breaks down, every time the lights go out, every time something doesn't work."

His lips pressed together into a flat line and he put his arms over his chest, but he didn't argue. She was right.

She took a deep breath, blowing it out, then deliberately turned her back on him to walk over to the table because she needed to tell him a little more. He was going to find out eventually, and it probably would be better for him to find out from her. If he made another trip, he might bring his brothers, and they might meet Shawn.

While Shawn seemed quite genial and didn't seem to have a temper, she didn't want the Emerson brothers ganging up on him and scaring him off.

Shawn didn't seem like the type that would scare easily either.

"We're getting married tomorrow," she said, just throwing the statement out there and letting it land wherever it would.

Heavy footsteps clomped across her kitchen floor, and they stopped right beside her.

She slowly straightened, pressing her tongue against her teeth and gripping the dishrag with clenched fingers.

"What did you say?"

"I said Shawn and I are getting married tomorrow."

"That's funny. No one in town has breathed a word about the wedding that you must be having. In the church? Where's the reception? At the fire hall?"

"Sarcasm doesn't become you, Braxton. Neither does beating around the bush. Just spit out what you're trying to say." Bridget's words were a little short, even though she wasn't exactly angry. Braxton was only trying to protect her.

Surely he understood she was only trying to do what was best for herself and her children.

"Marry me instead," he said, making it almost sound like he was saying, "I'll take the short end of the stick."

"First of all, you want to marry me just about as badly as you want to spend the entire summer picking rocks in your south forty. And second of all"—his lips quirked, but she ignored him—"and second of all, don't take this wrong, because I love you like a brother, but being married to you is a little bit repulsive. *Because* I love you like a brother." She crossed her arms over her chest and tapped her toe. Almost as though she were daring him to argue with her.

He didn't.

He understood exactly what she was saying. He didn't have anything but brotherly feelings for her, and a marriage between the two of them would be a business partnership and nothing else.

"Plus, Braxton, you once told me that you loved Arian's mother and she loved you. Has that changed?"

His lips tightened even more, and he shook his head slowly one time to the right, one time to the left.

His jaw bunched, but all of his frustration just made Bridget smile, because it only proved her right.

"Someday, she might come back." She held her hand up as he opened his mouth. "You don't have to tell me what the details are. But would it be fair of you to marry me when you love someone else?"

He blew out his breath and looked away.

"Not to mention, it wouldn't be fair of me to marry you when I know you love someone else. When I know there's someone else out there who loves you."

"Marry Preston, then. He'll take you."

"Oh. That's lovely. He'll take me, huh? Well, my goodness, aren't I the lucky one?"

"Sarcasm doesn't become you any better than it becomes me."

"I'm the queen of sarcasm. You are this dark, brooding, angry..."

He lifted his brows and lowered his head at her.

"Teddy bear. Soft and cuddly on the inside. You need to work on the outward manifestation of your inward teddy bear, though, because honestly, if I didn't know you, you'd scare me."

"That's good. I like that. Scary. That's me."

She was tempted to say maybe Arian's mother would come back if he weren't so scary, but she didn't know the details, and she didn't want to hit him where it hurt on accident.

She didn't want to marry him, but she definitely, most definitely, didn't want to hurt him. He was a good man, and whatever his issues were with Arian's mother, she hoped he worked them out sooner rather than later because he deserved a good woman.

"Not really. Everyone knows you're a teddy bear."

"Bridget." He ran a hand over his head in frustration. "I just don't want to see you hurt. None of us do. I happened to be the one that was in town at the feed store and heard about it. I'm sure my brothers are all gonna want to make a visit, if I can't talk them out of it."

"You can tell them they're wasting their time. I've met Shawn. I've worked with him. I know my dad must have liked and trusted him, and I know that if I don't do something with the farm, I'm going to have to sell it and move away. And you know why."

"That stupid curse. It's a crock of foolishness. Don't pay any attention to it."

"How can I not pay attention to it? People were trying to warn him from even coming here. No one in town will have anything to do with working with or for me. If I want to keep this farm, Shawn is my only choice."

"You mean people were warning him away?"

"Yes."

"They told him about all the deaths on the farm?"

"Yes."

"And he still came out? He still wants to marry you?"

"He does."

Braxton nodded slowly. The idea that Shawn wasn't being scared away by the townspeople impressed him. That was not hard to see.

But then his eyes narrowed. "How do you know he's not going to want to sell the farm as soon as you guys get married? Take the money and run."

"We're going to talk tomorrow about stipulations. I can put that in. But I'm sure he can also show me his accounts on his phone. He told me he just sold his farm, and that's why his dad told my dad he could come out for a bit—he didn't have any responsibilities of his own. But he wanted to buy a farm closer to his family. Apparently, the money he made from the farm that he sold is sitting in his account somewhere. He said he didn't need my money."

"It could be a lie," Braxton said, holding his chin between his thumb and his forefinger and rubbing thoughtfully over his short beard. "But like you said, you should be able to see his accounts tomorrow. Make sure you insist on it. And if he can't or won't show you, make sure there's something written up that the farm is yours no matter what happens."

She supposed there were people who would think she should get upset at Braxton's high-handed way of commanding her. But he was the eldest, bossy, and used to being obeyed. "That's kind of the plan that was forming in my head. That's what I'll do."

"Promise?" he asked, like they were kids again.

"I promise." She took a step forward and placed a hand on his arm. "You know I wouldn't do anything that I thought would endanger my girls in any way. They're more important to me than anything. Anything."

"I know. Just sometimes we get desperate, and we do things that aren't smart, things that we regret."

He didn't say any more. He really didn't need to. It was obvious he had some of those things in his past. Things that he did that he regretted.

"I appreciate your concern. I appreciate everything that you and your brothers have done for me. I guess I don't say that enough, but I should. You've been better to me than I deserve. And I owe you all, big time."

"You take care of my grandmother. She's feisty, and prickly at times, but she loves you, and all of us appreciate the time and effort that you put into making time for her, letting her be a part of your family as well as ours."

"How could I not? She was almost like a mom to me growing up. And she's been just as good to me as you guys have."

"All right, kid, if I can't talk you out of it, at least let me know if you ever need me, ever, for anything, and if that guy turns out to be a jerk especially, just say the word."

"I will, but I know I won't need to," she said, with more assurance than she felt.

He bent down to kiss her forehead and hadn't quite touched it when a throat cleared and a familiar, deep voice said, "Am I interrupting something?"

Chapter 11

Shawn stood just outside the screen door, watching a tall, dark man kiss the forehead of the woman he was to marry tomorrow.

It wasn't a passionate kiss. Not even close.

If he hadn't known that she was an only child, he might have thought the man was a brother. That, and they didn't look anything alike.

Still, Bridget jerked back when she heard him like she was guilty of doing something wrong. Her eyes were wide open when she turned to him.

"Shawn. I thought you'd left for the evening?" She even sounded guilty.

Or surprised.

The dark man put a hand on Bridget's shoulder, almost possessively, and Shawn narrowed his eyes at that before he looked back at Bridget.

"I had. But I heard something in town, and I wanted to run it by you."

"Oh?" she asked, like he was gonna stand outside the door and talk to her about personal matters while there was a stranger in the kitchen.

"I didn't realize you would be busy. I guess we'll just deal with whatever happens tomorrow."

He hadn't realized he'd have these feelings of possessiveness, because this was where he should turn and walk away, leaving her to her business.

But he didn't want to. Even though he didn't view the man as a threat, exactly, it didn't sit right with him to walk away while another man had his hand on the woman he was supposed to marry, nor did it sit right to leave them alone together.

He almost grunted, because he trusted her enough to say he would marry her tomorrow, but it was hard to walk away from her tonight. Not necessarily because he didn't trust her, but because... He wasn't sure.

He turned to leave, thinking that if he trusted her, he needed to show it. He also wasn't going to make this into a challenge as to which man she was going to choose.

She had no reason to choose Shawn anyway, since she barely knew him. And obviously whoever she was with knew her quite well.

He didn't want to compete against her friends, if that's what this man was.

He turned and had taken one step away from the door when Bridget called out, "Wait!"

He took another step and one more before he stopped.

He stood, looking at the steps, before he turned his head over his shoulder. "What?"

"What did you want?"

"It can wait 'til tomorrow."

"Obviously, you felt it was important enough to make another drive out here. Can you tell me?" she asked as she stopped on the other side of the screen door.

His eyes went from her to the man standing behind her. Other than turning to face him and crossing his arms over his chest, the man hadn't moved. He was as at home in Bridget's kitchen as he was anywhere.

"I wasn't planning on discussing it in front of an audience. We'll talk tomorrow."

"Shawn!"

He stopped but didn't turn back around.

"Excuse me," she said low, probably talking to the guy beside her, then the screen door opened.

The storm door closed, and then the screen door slapped shut.

"Is there something wrong?" she asked, appearing at his elbow.

He ground his teeth together, shoving a hand in his pocket.

He would have waited until tomorrow. It would have been too late for what he wanted, but he would have waited.

"It's fine. You have company. I didn't mean to interrupt you. Go on back." He put a foot down the first step.

"Seriously? You're angry because I was in the kitchen with a neighbor who's like a brother to me?"

That stopped him. And he turned.

"Do I look angry?" he asked.

"No. But you're acting like it."

"I just said we'd talk about it tomorrow. It's not that big a deal." Now it was a matter of whether or not he was going to do what she wanted, which was obviously tell her what he had wanted in the first place when he came.

Maybe he was a little annoyed, because there was just something in him that didn't want to give in.

He almost laughed. His parents had preached for years that marriage was a give-and-take. That it wasn't easy. That you had to work at it. That being married was fun but it was also hard. He'd always assumed it was big stuff, obvious stuff, and that he'd recognize it and want to stay married so badly that he'd be gracious and make sure he did the hard work they were talking about.

But maybe stuff like this—little stuff—was what they were talking about. Little stuff that added up to big stuff but that was hard to recognize when a person was living it.

When he wanted to do what he had originally intended, to walk away from her and not be swayed to do something different just because she'd demanded he talk to her.

He wanted to wait.

Maybe it was a simple thing, but wasn't that life?

Everything started out so simple, but disagreements grew into something bigger and bigger because no one was willing to give up what they wanted and let the other person "win."

He let out a breath. His parents also told him he couldn't keep score in a marriage. Because it wasn't about who gave up the most. All of life, including a marriage, was about dying to self and putting the other person first.

He wasn't even married, and already his parents' teachings were hammering in his head.

He turned and shoved a hand in his pocket, putting the other one on the porch post. "I met the jeweler coming out of the restaurant in town. I don't remember his name."

"Mr. Spickler," Bridget said, without hesitation.

"He saw me looking in the window of the jewelry shop, introduced himself, and mentioned that he was going to be away for the rest of the week. He asked me if there was something I wanted, saying that he lived above the jewelry shop, and he would open it anytime this evening if I wanted." He looked away across the yard to the chicken house, not willing to let her see his vulnerability. He'd wanted to please her. He made his voice sound flat and unemotional. "I figured if you wanted a ring for the ceremony tomorrow, we should pick it out tonight. That's all."

She stood on the porch, staring at him with her mouth open. It seemed to take her a little while to digest what he said. He wasn't sure why. It was pretty straightforward. He'd been looking for a ring for the girl he was going to marry. If she wanted him to get her one, they needed to do it tonight. There wasn't anything complicated about that.

But his jaw clamped shut, and his eyes widened as hers seemed to fill with tears.

A breeze, much cooler than the unusual heat of the day, rattled the dry corn leaves that were lying on the field that had been harvested beside the yard.

"You're going to give me a ring?"

"Isn't that what normally happens when you get married?"

"Wedding rings?"

"Yeah. It's like a symbol that you use to show that you're married. I think the circle represents something that doesn't end or something like that. I don't know. I never really got into the symbolism. But I know when I see a woman, I can look at her hand and know whether or not she's taken. That's what the wedding ring means to me. I want one. Because that's the message I'll be giving after tomorrow. I wanted one for you too." He swallowed, keeping his face expressionless, because he had wanted a little more. "And a diamond. Isn't it customary to have an engagement ring as well?"

She pulled both lips in and seemed to clamp down on them while she wrapped her arms around herself and turned away from him.

Maybe there was something in her past that had scarred her about wedding rings. He supposed it would be part of his job as her husband to handle her emotions or help her with them. That was another husband thing he wasn't sure he was going to be any good at.

He always hated it when his sisters got emotional.

"Forget about the rings. I didn't know it was going to upset you," he said, wishing he would have just gone with his first instinct and left without saying anything.

But then he would have upset her tomorrow. And even though theirs was a marriage of convenience, not exactly a love match, he wanted their wedding day to be a happy one.

"No. You didn't upset me," she said, the wobble in her voice making her words seem like a lie.

"Yeah. I guess it's something I gotta learn about you? That you're gonna cry over random statements?"

Maybe his words weren't the most considerate words in the world, but she was really making him uncomfortable with her sniffing and her struggle to contain her emotions.

"No. It's...not that," she began, but the sound of the door opening interrupted her.

"I feel like I'm trapped in your house. Is it okay if I leave? Or am I interrupting something?" The dark man opened the door and stepped out on the porch without waiting for anyone to answer him.

He was slightly taller than Shawn and a little broader through the shoulders, although Shawn's hand was just as work roughened as the man's when he held it out. "I'm Braxton. I guess Bridget should have introduced us, instead of running to you and slamming the door shut in my face. Never could teach that kid any manners."

"Shut up, Braxton. Weren't you leaving?" Bridget said. Although her words were a little harsh, there was nothing but affection in her voice.

Shawn definitely recognized the tight feeling in his throat as jealousy. She didn't have that kind of feeling in her voice when she talked to him.

She might never have it.

The thought came from nowhere; he wasn't sure what to make of it. He absolutely didn't like it though.

The idea of a marriage in name only sounded good. A marriage of convenience. But... He supposed now that he thought about it, he'd figured that if they didn't exactly fall in love with each other, there would be affection at the very least in their marriage.

Laughter.

Smiles.

Secret smiles.

Soft touches. Casual conversation and easy familiarity.

The idea that they might never have that wasn't one he wanted to think about.

Just because you're married doesn't mean you can't court her.

He hadn't processed that thought before Braxton said, "Braxton Emerson. I'm Bridget's neighbor."

"And self-appointed keeper, apparently," Bridget mumbled.

Shawn grabbed Braxton's outstretched hand. "Shawn Barclay. I'm Bridget's fiancé. We're getting married tomorrow."

"So I just heard," Braxton said, a little thoughtfully but with a crinkle in his eye that could almost be humor. "She had a lot of high words of praise for you."

"That's good to hear. Earlier, she had trouble coming up with anything."

"That's not true!" Bridget interrupted him.

He lifted his shoulder, tempted to quote what she'd said, but he didn't need to. Her eyes met his, and he could see the memory flash in her eyes.

Her mouth snapped closed, although her eyes widened. Maybe she hadn't realized the way her words had sounded, especially after he'd gone on, making quite a long list of wonderful things about her.

Braxton snorted. "She told me you were honest and upright, and that if her dad trusted you, then she would too." Braxton lifted a brow at Bridget who...Shawn almost thought if he weren't there, she would have stuck her tongue out at Braxton.

The thought was enough to curve his lips up a little.

"Wow. High words of praise indeed," Shawn said, with more than a little sarcasm in his voice.

"I think he has his work cut out for him." Braxton glanced at Bridget. Then he looked back at Shawn. "I came here because I was concerned about her. I'm leaving concerned about you. Don't let her walk all over you. She's pretty pushy."

"You can leave now," Bridget said, irritation mixed with the affection in her voice.

Braxton lifted a shoulder. "If you need some help, Shawn, or a shoulder to cry on, my brothers and I totally understand." He started toward the steps, jerking his head at Bridget. "See you later, kid."

"I think you better go rotate the lug nut covers on your tractor tires," Bridget called to his retreating back. "At least that should make you feel important, and it's a job simple enough for you to do."

Braxton kept walking down the walk, lifting his hand and waving, then throwing over his shoulder, "If you're looking for something to do, maybe you could *fix his haircut*." His words sounded like they should be punctuated by a stuck out tongue.

Shawn couldn't see if they were or not.

"So that's your brother?" Shawn asked, knowing he wasn't but wanting to know exactly what the relationship was, as Bridget glared at Braxton's retreating back.

"He might as well be. He has three brothers, and they live on the farm that adjoins ours to the south."

Shawn wasn't sure exactly what she meant by her use of the word "ours," but he liked the sound of it. It eased the irritation in his chest a little more.

She turned to face him. "I'm sorry if I sounded irritated. Usually, Braxton's the best of the bunch. But tonight...I don't know."

"He's just looking out for you."

"I'm glad you could see that. I was afraid you might be thinking that there was more than what there is between us."

"No." Shawn stared at her and finally said, "If there was more between you, he would not have been kissing your forehead."

Her breath hitched, and he wasn't sure why, only knew that his own breathing had become unsteady.

There was noise inside the house, a thump and some yelling.

"I better go see what's going on with the girls. You can come back in if you want to."

"No. I just didn't know what you thought about the rings."

"I don't think I'm going to be able to get away from the girls. I promised them I'd read to them, and then it's going to be bedtime. Would you mind picking something out?" Her lip slanted down, like she wished she could but was making the best decision for her kids.

Why did he feel disappointed? That had to be what the sinking, pulling feeling in his chest was, but he said, "Tell me a ring size. And what kind of ring do you want?"

She told him her size and then said, "Nothing fancy. I have to work with my hands, and I don't want to worry about keeping a fancy ring nice. I want something I can wear that I don't have to worry about."

He didn't know anything about rings, but he tucked that information away in his head and figured he could tell it to Mr. Spickler and hope the man would have an idea of what a woman wanted when she said something like that. Because Shawn had no clue.

"I'll see what he has. And I'll do my best."

"Shawn?"

"Yeah?"

"Thank you for telling me. I know we were kind of...butting heads about it, I guess. And I realized after you stopped and said what you did—what I was asking you to say—that you'd given in. And...I hope that's not the way it always is. Because a marriage shouldn't be just one person doing all the giving. It should be both of us." She lifted her brows as though asking him, although her words didn't contain any questions.

He shifted, stifling a laugh. "I agree. I was laughing a little to myself, because...my parents told me that marriage was hard. That it would require compromise. That sometimes you didn't get your way, and sometimes it felt like you were the only one giving, but if you're determined to stay married, you'd keep giving." This time, he did chuckle a little. "I guess that was a little premarital practice. It's helped me to open my eyes a little as to what exactly they meant. In my youthful naivety, I always pictured marriages as all fun and games, and the idea that it might be hard was for other people, not me."

She stared at him as the seconds ticked by. He almost opened his mouth to ask if he had a fly in his nose, when she said, "I think...I think if both of us have that attitude, there's no way our marriage couldn't not work."

He nodded. "I'm pretty sure that's what my parents were thinking too. I wish I could say that I picked you on purpose because I knew that's how you felt as well, but it's just a welcome piece of information, nothing I deserve or chose."

"Me too." She bit her lip. "If you want to come in, I'll fix your haircut."

He hesitated. It had already been a big day for her. But...he didn't want to leave. He enjoyed her company, but there was something more. Something that pulled at him and made him want more. More of her time. More of her smiles. More of her standing there looking at him like she might like him a little. Or a lot.

"I don't want it to be a bother."

"It's not. Tomorrow's your first wedding. Maybe you'll want to look good for it?"

"Ha. I'm a man. I don't care about my hair. But I don't want to embarrass you."

"You're not going to embarrass me, but maybe someone will take our picture and eventually the girls might care that you looked like you had a lopsided mohawk on our wedding day."

"You think?"

"Girls are funny like that."

"Then, yeah. I'll come back in and you can cut it. For the girls."

They smiled at each other, and something tripped in Shawn's chest. Sweet and warm and good.

He followed her into the house and waited while she settled an argument and sent the girls off to get baths.

She pulled out a pair of clippers.

"That seems like an odd thing for a mother of all girls to have." He shouldn't have said anything, but he couldn't help his curiosity about her previous husbands.

"Neither Patrick nor Blade would let me cut their hair, but dad always wanted me to. He hated going to the barbershop."

"I see. I don't hate going to the barbershop..." Except he didn't care for the men's conversation.

"Obviously. That's why you left with half a haircut." Her words were dry.

"Right. I didn't used to hate going to the barbershop."

She had the clippers out and ready. Pointing to a chair, she waited until he sat down.

"I think this is the right size." She hesitated with the clippers poised over his head. "I can't really tell if there was something specific going on here, or if he was just clipping it all..."

"Whatever you do is fine. It's just hair. Most of it will grow back."

"Most?" She chuckled.

"It's not quite as thick as it used to be."

"Whether or not a man has hair isn't a mark of character," she said, switching the clippers on and beginning to cut with the confidence of someone who'd done it many times before.

"Good thing, or I'd be in a bad way."

"Character isn't something you lack."

He took that as a compliment, but didn't say anything.

Her hands on his head were sure, but gentle. He was tempted to close his eyes and enjoy, but she moved closer, her body graceful and so very different from his. He found himself pressing his hands onto his legs, resisting the odd urge to touch her.

It felt like forever and not nearly long enough when she switched the clippers off and stood back, her eyes roving over his head, checking out her handiwork.

"I pass inspection?" he said, uncomfortable with just sitting. Wanting to move, to get closer, walk away, ease the aching irritation that made him want to squirm.

"Nope. Missed a spot right here." She touched a spot beside his temple. "I always missed it on dad, too." She glanced at him as she spoke. Their eyes caught as her voice trailed off. Her hands stilled and she seemed to barely breathe. His own breath felt shallow and too fast.

Her tongue touched her lip and his eyes dropped. His heart swung wildly, slapping against his ribs.

"I...I'd better get it," she whispered.

He watched each movement of her lips, the full curve of the bottom, the heart-shaped bow of the top, and couldn't seem to tear his eyes away. Didn't want to.

He swallowed, his throat dry and tight, wanting to tell her that she was beautiful. That she had character, too. That he admired her and was fascinated by her and would work however long and hard he had to, do whatever it took to protect her and her girls and keep them safe and happy.

"Bridget, I...I want-"

"Mommy? Are you going to read to us?"

Their heads both jerked to Portia, standing in the doorway in her nightgown, standing in little bare feet with her hair still wet.

Bridget seemed to shake herself and she squeaked, "Yes." She cleared her throat and tried again. "Yes. I will be right there."

She was all business as she snapped the clippers on and snipped off the hair she'd missed the first time.

"There. You're all done." Her pulled back smile didn't reach her eyes.

"Thanks. Tell me where the broom is and I'll take care of the mess. You can go read to the girls."

She told him the location of the broom and almost seemed to sigh with relief as he took the clippers from her hand.

"Thanks for cleaning up," she said.

He jerked his chin up. "I'll see you in the morning."

She nodded, her face thoughtful. "In the morning."

Chapter 12

Shawn sat on the back of his pickup, one leg pulled up and his forearm resting on it, leaning against the side wall, his other leg dangling down.

He held his phone to his ear and waited for his dad to answer, looking up at the wide-open Iowa sky. Filled with stars, twinkling and beautiful.

The wind stirred the dry leaves of corn in the field beside him with a raspy sound, bringing the deep, fragrant smell of clean, resting earth to his nose. A good smell. Pure and right and familiar, even if he'd only smelled it in Arkansas before.

He'd stopped at a random deserted spot along the road about thirty minutes from Bridget's farm, brown cornfields stretching on either side in the daylight, but now, in the dark and cold, they were just big, empty blobs of black.

There were no hotels in Prairie Rose, and the closest one was another ten minutes away.

But he hadn't felt like going to the hotel just yet, wanting to be alone.

This seemed like as good a place as any.

"Shawn?" his dad answered.

"Hey, Dad."

"You make it to Iowa okay?"

"I did. I met Bridget."

"I see." There was a pause. "What did you think of her?"

That seemed like an odd question for his dad. Shouldn't he have been asking what he thought of the farm? Wasn't that what he was supposed to be helping with? Interesting that his dad was asking about Bridget.

"I'm going to marry her tomorrow."

That should answer his dad's question.

He kinda figured his dad would be quiet for a while, so he didn't look to see if he dropped the call when he met dead silence on the line. Instead, he leaned his head back up, picking out the Big Dipper and Orion's belt.

He'd found the Little Dipper and was working on the North Star when his dad finally spoke.

"You know, Shawn, that of all your siblings, you're the one that is the jokester. And I could see you thinking about why I might have sent you there, figuring it out, and messing with me about it. But I don't think that's the case."

"It's not. I didn't figure things out until I was sitting here listening to the phone ring."

"You don't sound angry."

"How could I be? My siblings are all happy. Deliriously happy in some instances, if not all. You and Mom knew exactly what they needed...who they needed. Even as I was figuring it out, I had to applaud you. I think you made a good choice in my instance as well."

"But?" his dad said, as though hearing that word in his tone.

"I'm a little annoyed at myself for not figuring it out."

His dad chuckled. Then he sobered. "How did you get her to agree so fast? Did you tell her that your parents were experts, and she should just trust them? Oh, wait, you couldn't have since you just figured it out."

"Did you know about the curse?"

His dad took a breath and then held it for a few seconds before saying, "Yeah. Her dad told me about it. I think it's what kept him living so long after the accident. He was fighting it as hard as he could because he knew what the town would say when he passed."

"I see. Aren't you afraid you might lose me?" Shawn asked, supposing he ought to be upset that his parents might have sent him into a dangerous situation on purpose.

Maybe he should think they didn't care about him or wanted him to die, but that was nonsense, and he wasn't afraid to say so. He certainly wouldn't allow himself to think anything different.

"I didn't figure you'd put any more credence in that than I did. Or than her dad did."

"You're right. Unfortunately, she believes it."

"Yeah. After losing two husbands and her brother, she was wavering. But then her dad passed, and that probably sent her over the edge."

"I don't know what to do about it. The town's adamant about it. She said even her girls believe it."

"All you have to do is live," his dad said simply.

"Well, I've been doing that okay for thirty years. But there's always the chance that something could happen."

For the first time, the idea of his death shot fear through him. Not at the idea of dying. He'd come to terms with that a long time ago, although of course he didn't want to. But he hadn't been afraid. Now? Now if something happened to him, Bridget would almost be assured of the curse.

And it could devastate her. Possibly ruin her for the rest of her life.

"What's the matter, son?" his dad asked, almost as though he could see the thoughts that were knocking around in his brain.

He had to get a handle on them, or he'd talk himself out of tomorrow.

"If something happens to me, you need to take care of Bridget."

He couldn't even believe he was asking his dad to take care of a woman he hadn't even married yet.

"She'll have plenty of money," his dad said.

It was almost as though his dad was testing him.

"You know that's not what I meant."

"I know. I guess I was surprised at the worry in your voice."

"Yeah, me too. It shouldn't be there."

"God has this, son."

"I know. It just takes faith. Faith over fear." He grinned. "I'm quoting my dad."

"I heard that."

"Funny. You should have heard me earlier today, talking to myself. I was repeating the marriage lecture you always gave us. The one where you said it was hard, you had to work for it, and you had to give things up, give up your way...you know, the 'love is not selfish' one."

"I thought you said you weren't getting married until tomorrow?"

"I know. It's pretty bad if I'm using the marriage advice before the actual marriage."

"No, that's good. I want you to stay married. And I think I'd say your marriage has a pretty good chance when you haven't even known your wife-to-be for more than a day, but it's what you're talking about right there that makes a marriage last. It really has nothing to do with how long you've been together, or how old you are, or how different you might be, or how in love you consider yourself. Having a marriage last comes down to being willing to give up what you want for the benefit of the person you're married to. And being willing to do that over and over again. Commitment and perseverance."

"And keeping your eyes on your spouse," Shawn said dryly, knowing that was part of commitment. A man couldn't look around at other women if he wanted to stay committed to the woman he was married to.

"So you *were* listening. Shock my socks off," his dad said, the humor clear in his tone.

"I should be offended at that, but I can't be. I wouldn't have thought I was listening either. But somehow, it got in there, and I'm glad. It's made me wiser."

"Than the average bear," his dad added.

"Thanks for taking the time to teach me, Dad. I know you had to say a bunch of things over and over and over again, and you probably wondered if I was ever going to get it. But I appreciate it now. I don't think I thank you nearly like I should."

"I suppose it's always nice to be appreciated, but I'm proud of the man you've become. And I don't say that nearly as much as I should."

His dad's words made the back of his throat tighten up. He knew his dad loved him. Knew his dad was proud of him and pleased with what he had become.

He tried as hard as he could to walk in such a way that not just his earthly father would be proud of him, but his Heavenly Father would be pleased as well. Sometimes, it meant he lost friends. Sometimes, it meant people made fun of him. Sometimes, it meant he stood alone.

But always in Arkansas, he had his family nearby. Sure, his farm had been farther away than he wanted it, but it hadn't been states away.

Now, he had this town to face and their determination that there was a curse on his wife-to-be, and he had to figure out some way to convince them it wasn't so.

And he had to do it by himself.

"You're not alone," his dad said, almost as though he could read his mind.

"I know."

God was with him.

"It's funny, of all my siblings, why am I the one that had to leave?"

"God has different trials for everyone. It's really not up to us to question them. It's just up to us to do the very best we can through them."

"You know if I do this, get married tomorrow, I'm never coming back to Arkansas?"

"Never say never. But yeah, I knew when I sent you out that that was a distinct possibility. And trust me, I didn't want to."

Would he have left if he had known that he would never be going home again? Not more than for short visits?

Even as he asked himself that question, he knew the answer. He had been sure, one hundred percent sure, that it was God's will for him to be in Iowa.

That hadn't changed.

If he had the faith that he claimed he had, he would still have gone. Just like he was still going to stay. Just like he was still going to get married tomorrow.

"I kinda wish you and Mom could be here, even though I know it's not going to be a very big affair."

"Your mom and I can come out if you want."

"No. It's probably going to last about fifteen minutes. There's no point in driving so many hours, just to stand here for a few minutes. I just wanted you to know I wanted you here."

"Good to know, son. It's always nice to be wanted."

They chatted a little bit about the farm, and Shawn told his dad about the chicken house while his dad told him what he knew about his friend and the plans he'd had for the farm.

Shawn made a note to talk to Bridget about them and see what she thought. But probably not tomorrow. Although, he would like to have a tour of the farm so he could get in his head what all needed to be done.

He and his dad hung up, and he let his hand drop to the bed of the truck as he sat there, his eyes on the stars, his mind whirling with the changes in his life.

Not a single car had gone by.

It almost seemed like the state shut down at nine o'clock.

Not a bad thing.

He would miss his family for sure, and there was hurt in his heart at the idea that he wouldn't be a part of all of the big family celebrations, birthdays, holidays, and all of the other things that families got together and celebrated.

But, on the other hand, Bridget seemed to have her own ready-made family here. Not just her girls, but her neighbors as well. And maybe, if he could disabuse the town of the notion that she was cursed, maybe he would find his new family right here, in Prairie Rose, Iowa.

Chapter 13

The next morning, Shawn was already in the chicken barn when Bridget and Robin walked in.

"Good morning," he greeted them from the control room where he was grabbing the numbers that she had shown him and writing them down in the daily log.

"Good morning," she echoed, pushing back against her rioting stomach. Shawn looked just as good as she remembered in his jeans and boots, his face friendly and open. Her heart twirled, and her hands started to sweat. "I never thought to ask if you'd like me to bring you coffee," she said, holding up the cup she carried. "I didn't know if you were a coffee drinker."

He wrinkled his nose.

"Does that change things?" she asked, knowing it wouldn't.

"I don't know. I might have to think about that." He flashed a grin at her, making sure she saw that he was joking before he turned back and wrote some more numbers down.

Robin had gone over and started the belt, beginning to pack eggs while Bridget waited for Shawn to finish writing and look up again. His hands, strong and sure, fascinated her, and she had to remind herself not to stare.

"Did you want to walk around and get the floor eggs? Or did you want to pack with Robin?" Her voice sounded surprisingly normal, considering the inner turmoil she was having a hard time controlling.

"You tell me what you want me to do." He set the pen down and walked out of the control room.

"How about you go around and pick up the floor eggs. That's the harder job. That basket is really heavy in the morning."

He nodded, grabbing the basket and walking out into the barn.

He didn't say much when he came back in, washing the eggs and doing everything that she had shown him yesterday. Eventually, she sent Robin back down to the house to get ready for school and make sure her sisters were ready, and they packed eggs in silence.

Whether he was as nervous as she was, she couldn't tell, but she couldn't deny that her stomach was churning, and her chest felt tight almost to the point of pain.

She also dropped seven eggs, when normally she dropped one, if that.

The night before, they hadn't had to move any skids around, and it took a little longer as she showed him how to use the skid jack and pack the skids in the big walk-in cooler.

By the time they got down to the house, the girls were ready for school. Portia sat at the table with a bowl of cereal.

"If you don't mind, I'm going to go change my clothes, and I think I have time to grab a quick shower."

If he thought it was funny that she was being vain, he didn't say. But if they truly were going to get married today, she didn't want to do it in dirty clothes.

The girls were subdued, maybe uncomfortable with the stranger in their midst, although they seemed to be accepting him okay. Robin might have been the most standoffish, but that was to be expected. Maybe she felt like she didn't want to get attached because according to the curse, Shawn wouldn't be around long.

It wasn't just Bridget who had lost so many people in her life.

By nine o'clock, they had dropped the girls off at school, gone to the diner and ordered food, and were sitting at the corner table way in the back.

The silence between them felt awkward, but she wasn't sure how to start the conversation.

He didn't seem bothered by the awkward silence, looking just as cool and collected as he had every time she'd seen him, except for the bit of anger he'd shown about the curse.

"Those eggs and sausage are a little bit of a step up from the watermelon you had yesterday." She nodded at his plate, grateful her voice didn't tremble.

"Hey, don't knock the watermelon. I read an article once where the reporter was interviewing a centurion. He said the secret to his longevity was that he ate watermelon every day. I figured it couldn't hurt."

"Wow. Maybe you shouldn't believe everything you read."

"Maybe you shouldn't believe everything the town tells you," he fired right back at her.

Her cheeks heated. It was an unusual feeling to have such a strong defender in her corner.

Of course, her father had been on her side, but he'd been more of a live and let live kind of person. He hadn't seemed to be as determined as Shawn was to fight things.

"Maybe you're going to get tired of defending me every second of every day."

She hadn't missed how Sadie at the cash register had given Shawn a pitying glance, shaking her head sadly.

Shawn had to have seen it, too.

"No. I don't think so. Defending you is a privilege. It's something I'm taking on willingly. And planning to relish. Because I'm going to win."

He gave her a carefree smile, and before she could think about it, he had her smiling in return. His words almost made her forget about the notebook she had in her purse.

She reached over and grabbed it, setting it on the table and opening it up to the page where she'd written the things that were important to her for their marriage.

When she looked up, Shawn's brows were raised.

"Looks like someone did some thinking overnight."

"They weren't second thoughts, I promise." Then she bit her lip. "You didn't have second thoughts?"

"Yeah, I did have to come to terms with the idea that Iowa would be my home. I've never even considered living anywhere but Arkansas. I guess I should do a full disclosure and say a piece of my heart will always be there."

"As long as the piece you leave there isn't necessary to sustain life, I suppose it's okay."

They grinned, even though his words made her sad. That was the second time he'd given up for her, without asking her for a compromise, without saying anything. Just knew that they couldn't both have what they wanted, and so he gave to her and didn't ask for a thing in return.

"I know we're not supposed to be keeping score, but you're winning by two points," she murmured, looking at the notebook page she had filled with all the things that she wanted to say to him.

"I'm not keeping score. I'm not even thinking that way."

"I know." She looked at the notebook again.

She had wanted to see his bank account. See that he had the money he said he had.

Ask him to sign something that would guarantee that once they were married, he wouldn't sell the farm. Nor try to talk her into selling it.

A guarantee that they would live in Iowa forever. On the farm.

She had even split the chores on the farm, making him agree that he would do the fieldwork and leave her in charge of the chicken barn. She figured he wouldn't have any problem with that, since yesterday was the first time he'd ever been in one, and she had been running it for years.

But she wanted those guarantees.

She wanted to know that she wasn't making a mistake and that their bases were covered.

There was more, too.

That he would agree not to make her say that she would obey him in their marriage vows. After all, she barely knew him. How could she agree to obey?

She tapped the notebook with her finger. She'd also written that half of their possessions would be hers. That she had sole say in the raising of her girls. That he would never hit her, that if he ever cheated on her or left her, he would give her half the money that he brought into their marriage.

All things that benefited her. And there were more.

Slowly, she closed the notebook.

"Now you're scaring me. What's that look for?" His eyes went to her notebook as she put it in her purse. "And what are you doing putting that away? I thought we were going to talk?"

"No. No."

Suddenly, the bacon and eggs in front of her didn't look appetizing as she thought about how selfish she had been about their marriage. The way she looked at it had been solely about her.

Not that she thought that she should go into it with her eyes closed, but it was a sobering moment and not her proudest one to know that her main concern had been her and her interest, and if she had gone through with the things in the notebook, she was almost certain that Shawn would have allowed her, given her whatever she wanted, even if it meant he had to give up more. When he'd already given up so much.

Not to mention, he'd already defended her, he'd put himself in harm's way, pitted himself against the entire town, just to be sitting here with her this morning, and all that would be multiplied by more after he'd said "I do."

"Then what is it?" he asked softly. "Do you have it memorized?" A gently teasing note entered his tone.

"No."

"Well then, go ahead, hit me with everything you got." He leaned his head down, trying to catch her eye and maybe get a smile.

She couldn't do it. Just couldn't. All her demands, her questions, the things she had to make sure of...it wasn't right. None of it. Not when he would be the only one giving up.

But...she took a breath. "There's only one thing. Do you have any references?" That was for the safety of her children. It wasn't about her, and she wouldn't allow it to be, but she did have a responsibility to make sure that he was exactly what he seemed, even though he'd pretty much proved it in the last twenty-four hours.

He pulled his phone out of his pocket and handed it across the table. "This is my password," he said, rattling off a few numbers.

"What am I supposed to do with that?"

"Read my texts. Check out my social media. You can call anyone in my contact list. Ask them about me. Some of my contacts are sales and repair people, from the farm, but most are family and friends. I'm sure any one of them will tell you whatever they can about me. Call anyone."

Unless he'd spent the entire night calling everyone on his contact list warning them that someone might be calling and they should say good things about him, this was about the best thing he could do to allow her to see if he was who he seemed to be.

"Do you want my phone?" she asked, a little uncertain. She'd not expected such transparency. She thought he'd give her a list of the people most likely to say good things, and she'd make a few phone calls.

"No. I talked to my dad last night. I don't need anything else."

She swallowed, nodding then taking a breath and looking down at her plate.

"I guess I'll call your dad, if that's okay," she said, looking back up.

"Anyone you want."

If it weren't for her kids, she would have handed the phone back. But she couldn't just do that without at least making sure he was who he said he was.

In his contacts, his dad was simply "dad." She punched the number and put the phone to her ear.

"Shawn?" A male voice came on the line, articulate and compassionate, even through the phone.

"No. It's Bridget," she said.

"Ah, Bridget. How are you?" the man said, sounding like he truly cared how she was.

"I'm fine. But I asked Shawn for references... I suppose he told you that we're getting married today?"

"Yeah. I talked to him last night."

"You knew my dad?"

"I did." Race went on a little bit, talking about her dad and saying things that proved to Bridget that he was actually good friends with him. It eased her mind, knowing he was what Shawn had said he was and what she had thought he was as well.

"Is there anything else I can do for you?" Race finally said.

"I guess... I guess if it weren't for my daughters, I wouldn't be calling you at all. But I feel like I need to make sure that Shawn is what he says he is, for their safety."

"Of course. I hope Shawn appreciates that. It's not every mother that puts her children first."

"I think he does. I know he does. In every interaction we've had, he's put me first." Her eyes met Shawn's across the table as she spoke.

A little bit of surprise entered into them as he listened to her compliment. Maybe they smiled some as the surprise melted into something that looked like affection and that stirred something in her. Something warm and good. Something that felt right.

"He's a good man. Not a perfect man, and not a man that can't make mistakes or do stupid things. Because we all do. But your dad wanted the very best for you. He loved you with a deep, abiding love, and his heart ached over the pain you've suffered. As we talked, we knew that Shawn could be perfect for you." Race seemed to hesitate, then he continued. "He's quick to laugh. Quick to joke, but he works hard, and the laughter and the joking mask a tender heart. One that's easily hurt but also a giving heart. He'd give his very soul for the people he loves. And the fact that he's willing to give up his family says a lot. As for your girls, I can assure you, you don't have anything to worry about. He's loyal and protective, and you might have to be patient while he learns the parenting ropes, but he will make a good father."

Bridget held the phone to her ear as Mr. Race said everything she already knew in her heart. She nodded, even though he couldn't see her, in agreement with his words.

Shawn would be a good husband and father. That's all she needed to know.

They'd work everything else out.

After they said a few more words, she hung up and handed the phone back to Shawn, who had finished his plate of food and was eyeing hers.

She glanced down at the food she still had no desire to eat, even though she wasn't nearly as upset and nervous as she had been when she entered the diner. "Do you want it?"

"Sure," he said easily, taking the plate and ignoring the phone.

"I was actually talking about your phone."

"Oh! I'm sorry." He started pushing the plate back.

"No, you can have that. I guess I'm too nervous to eat."

"Nervous?"

"Kind of a big step."

He laughed. "Please don't take this the wrong way, but this is your third time. I'm the one that should be nervous. I've never done this before."

"Really? You're gonna rub that in?"

He lifted a shoulder. "If the shoe fits." He smirked, then a look of consternation crossed his face. "Oh!" He shoved a bite of food in his mouth and reached into his front pocket, scrunching down in the booth seat, stretching his long legs out. "I talked to Mr. Spickler after I left you last night and picked out something I hope will be acceptable." He seemed to realize he was rambling on a little and stopped himself. He pulled out a small bag. "Go ahead and look at them," he said as he pushed the bag across the table to her.

She hadn't expected today to be such an emotional day. She took a trembling breath as she reached for the bag carefully.

"I promise it's not going to explode."

"You sound like you've said that before."

"I might have. But I mean it this time."

She laughed, although maybe it was a little nervous laugh. Still, his dad said he was goofy, and that was new for her. Neither one of her first two husbands had been goofy in the slightest.

One serious and scholarly, the other serious and buff.

She hadn't ever thought to wish for a man who could make her laugh. But she found it to be nice.

"I don't think I want to know the story behind that statement," she said as she pulled two boxes out of the bag.

"Yeah. You'll probably hear it though. Next time you meet my brothers."

She looked up at him under her lashes. "It sounds like your brothers might be good for blackmail."

His mouth was full, but his eyes twinkled. He swallowed before he said, "Indeed. Maybe I'll have to tell them the curse is transferable."

He was teasing, and even though she might have been a little bit sensitive about the whole curse thing, he'd been so adamant about not believing it she had to laugh and accept the fact that he was going to joke about it.

"If it's transferable, I can probably double it."

"That ought to be interesting. I think I can only die once, right?"

"You better not die at all. That was in my notebook. I die first."

"No. I think I'm gonna fight you on that one. And since the score is two to zero, you need to get some points on the board, my lady."

Lady? The Emerson brothers called her kid. The townspeople called her the Bad Luck Widow. Her dad had called her Gadget.

But Lady...? It was terrible that she would get emotional over a nickname. But it was a name that a man might call his wife, call the woman he...was fond of.

She liked that he was treating her like that.

Her hands paused as she considered the nickname, and she barely realized it.

Shaking her head, bringing her mind back to the present, she started opening the larger of the two boxes.

It held both of their wedding bands. His bigger and thicker than hers, both of them plain gold.

"I didn't want it so thick and heavy it was going to yank you to the bottom of the river if you fell in, but I wanted it big enough so people didn't have to squint to see it, to tell whether or not you belonged to me."

Whoa. The idea of belonging to someone.

She'd never really thought of marriage that way, but the opposite was also true. He had said he wanted a wedding band so people knew he was taken.

"And you belong to me," she said low and soft.

One side of his lip curved up in that endearing smile. The one that made her unable to do anything but smile back. "Look at the other one," he prompted.

"I think you're nervous," she said.

"I am. Mr. Spickler assured me that you would like this. He told me that you'd grown up in town, and he knew you as well as anyone."

That was true. Mr. Spickler went to her church and had taught the youth group with his wife.

If anyone knew her, he and his wife did.

"Are you drawing this out on purpose just to see how impatient you can make me or to see what kind of patience I have, or are you scared?" Shawn asked as he shifted in his seat.

"Sorry," she said, grinning at him, because he really was nervous. She wasn't making fun of that. It was just nice to know she wasn't the only one.

She took the box and opened the lid. It didn't take more than a second or two to know that the ring was perfect. Perfect for her. It was small and unpretentious but woven intricately, with the value in the skill of artistry and the presentation and not in the size of the stone.

"Mr. Spickler was right. This is perfect for me."

"You know, when he showed me what was in his case, this is the one that stood out to me, that really spoke your name, so when he pointed it out, it was a no-brainer for me."

"You know your dad said that your easygoing exterior hid a tender heart. I think he might have been right."

In her experience, it was unusual that he would even think of a ring, let alone get one that was so perfect. It wasn't typical male behavior.

She certainly was happy to know that she was getting a man who was thoughtful and considerate as well as funny.

She put a finger on the ring, touching it gently. "You're starting to make me feel like I'm getting the better end of this deal, and you're really not getting much of anything."

"Quit feeling like that, because it's not true. I don't know what would prompt you to say that. You're taking a big leap of faith today, and I'm just gonna do my level best to make sure you're not disappointed and there aren't any regrets. Ever."

"I'm pretty sure that's something you don't need to worry about."

He just grinned, then nodded his head at her ring. "You can try it on, but Mr. Spickler said it probably wouldn't fit. He'll need to size it, and that will take a few days. The wedding band, on the other hand, he had in your size and mine."

"They're the important things."

"I guess. Although I think the hand that wears it is the most important."

"You better be careful, I'll start thinking you're romantic on top of everything else." It could be dangerous for her heart. She hadn't been thinking that they would get too emotionally entangled.

Not that she minded. The problem was she didn't want to be the only one. If they were going to get their emotions involved, she wanted him to be just as infatuated with her as she was with him.

Otherwise, she could end up with a lot of pain, which couldn't be good for their marriage. It was better for her to be aloof and protect herself from falling in love, because that was one pain she'd never experienced in her life: unrequited love.

"Deep thoughts?" Shawn asked as he scraped up the last of the egg from her plate.

"Not really. I guess I'm just thinking I'm ready to go do this if you are."

"Now that I've finished up your breakfast, I'm ready to go," he said with a grin.

They slid out of the booth. Shawn grabbed the ring boxes while she gathered up their plates.

Silently, they threw their garbage away and walked out the diner door, heading down the street to the small church where they were to meet the pastor and their future.

Chapter 14

Bridget twisted the ring on her finger as Shawn and she walked toward the machinery shed on their farm. The wedding had been short. But not really sweet.

The pastor had at least not tried to talk Shawn out of it. That was a saving grace.

Although Shawn had said he'd been on the phone with him the night before. Maybe he'd tried to talk Shawn out of it then.

Whatever. It didn't matter.

Miss Matilda had been their witness, and that had been the best part of it.

Maybe not the very best part. Shawn had surprised her with his hooded gaze that she might have termed smoldering in a different context, in a different couple, in a different situation.

He almost acted like he really wanted to marry her, like they were going to have a real marriage, a real relationship, and he was excited to get started about it.

Maybe he was just playing his part, the part of his one-man crusade to convince the town that she wasn't cursed.

Whatever he was doing or thinking, it had made something that she thought she was going to have to endure a little exciting.

He had taken her hand, and she'd been surprised by the jolt of attraction.

That had been unexpected.

But the end of the short ceremony had been a letdown, because when the pastor had said he could kiss the bride, Shawn had given her a very clinical peck on the forehead. Similar to what the Emerson brothers might have given her.

At least he didn't say, "Thanks, kid."

He'd seemed a little flustered as he pulled back and met her eyes.

Maybe he'd seen the disappointment that she tried to hide.

Not that she wanted to go around kissing strangers, but...that had been something on her list. Something maybe they should have talked about before they actually went to the ceremony was hammering out what exactly their marriage was going to entail from the relationship angle.

Sometime today, they were gonna have to have that awkward conversation.

She wasn't in any rush though, and she supposed if she handed him his sheets and blankets and told him he could pick one of the two empty bedrooms, that might be all she needed to say.

Problem was she wasn't sure that's exactly how she wanted to handle it.

Opening the main door into the machine shed and flipping on the big fluorescent lights, she stepped inside, and Shawn followed her closely.

"This is where most of the equipment is over the winter. This is also where all of the tools are that we have for fixing things."

Shawn stopped beside her and looked around the building. She did not need to point out the tractors—a smaller one with a bucket on it and a larger one with dual wheels in the back and four-wheel drive.

"No combine?" Shawn asked, his eyes searching the room.

"We have one. It's parked out back in the shed. It needed some work done to it, and my brother was the one who did most of the work." She didn't allow her voice to trail off or be sad. Her brother had been gone for eight years, and although his death had been a blow, it was just one of the many she'd endured during her lifetime. "All of his tools and stuff are still here, but there hasn't been too much repair work going on. When something breaks and can't be slapped back together good enough to work, we hire a professional."

"I see. Sounds like I've got my work cut out for me."

"You do that kind of work?"

"A good bit of it. There are a few things I wouldn't touch, things that need to be precision cut, and I'm not the best welder in the world, although I see you've got a MIG welder over there in the corner. Might see if I can brush up on some things."

"My brother loved that kind of stuff. It wasn't farming that he really enjoyed, but he was more into the tractors and machinery and equipment. He and my dad got along beautifully with my dad loving the fieldwork and crops, keeping detailed records of everything he planted in every field, right down to the type and amount of fertilizer he put on everything."

"And you were the animal person."

"I am. I guess the three of us worked really well together."

"Yeah. It's funny how God works family out like that where people complement each other."

She knew her eyes were fluttering, but she barely noticed. Because she had never thought about it before.

"You're right. I guess I thought it was just coincidence, but...I suppose the Lord does tend to bring people together who complement each other."

"Friends and coworkers, of course, but often within the same family. I know people look at my brothers and me, and they can't tell us apart sometimes, especially when we were younger. But while we might look the same, we all have different strengths. When we're together, we make each other look good, because our strengths cover our weaknesses, and we're all able to contribute something different to whatever we're working on."

"I'm sorry you had to leave them behind."

"When God opens a door, you're foolish if you don't walk through."

"Foolish? He gives us free choice. You don't have to walk through when He opens the opportunity up for you." Honestly, she thought Shawn might have been better off walking away from their marriage. Because not only was he stuck in Iowa away from his family, but instead of buying the farm of his dreams near his parents and siblings, he had walked into a place that needed a lot of work and hadn't been kept up for years. Things decayed quickly when no one took care of upkeep or maintenance.

But Shawn didn't seem to care. His words were on a different subject.

"Sure. God tells us He wants to bless us. He wants to give us good things. He's our father. I can't imagine my dad looking at me and saying 'I don't want the best for you.' How much more does God look at us and want good things for us? The problem is our perspective is an earthly perspective, whereas He's looking down seeing the entire story and seeing that once we go through this little hard thing, or give up this thing that we really want, or walk through a situation that we're not sure we are going to be happy about and, *then*, it will open up all sorts of avenues for blessing, and our life will be richer and fuller and happier because of it. The problem is we often turn our back on those open doors because it looks too hard, or because we think we'll have to give up too much, or because it's scary to step out into something that might be a failure."

"People do fail. That's a fact of life." She agreed with most of what he was saying, but a person couldn't discount that sometimes things failed.

"And failure doesn't kill you."

She looked away. That was true. Plus... "Failure makes you stronger, if you let it."

"Exactly. And God knows that. Sometimes, He leads us through a door that results in failure. It's failure that we would have avoided if we had avoided the open door, but we would have avoided the lessons - lessons that make us better people. More compassionate people. People who see things from others' perspectives and notice things that we might not have known before. Just a whole wealth of experiences and ideas and attitudes and actions that we learn when things don't go the way we want them to."

Bridget tried not to look stunned. Everything that he was saying could be applied to her life hundreds of times over. All the hard things that she'd had to go through. All the deaths, the years of being a single mom. The whispers of the town, which had finally turned into outright openly accusing her of having a curse.

All of those things; she could get bitter over them, she could believe that there was a problem with her, or she could allow those things to shape and mold her into a wise and compassionate person who could help other people and show empathy that she didn't have even ten years ago.

"Of all my wedding days, this one was the least romantic." She laughed a little. "How many people can say 'of all my wedding days?'"

"It's your last one. Better enjoy it."

"It's been my least romantic, but...I feel like my eyes have been opened in so many different ways. I hadn't considered the things I've been through...You shifted the lens that I've been using to look at my life. In a good way."

He grunted. "I didn't realize it was a competition to see which husband could be the most romantic. Now that I know, I guess I need to work a little harder."

"That's not really the kind of marriage we have," she said, laughing a little and turning away.

As she turned, she caught the expression on his face. It had gone from easy congeniality to something that looked an awful lot like hurt.

Had Shawn expected more?

She wanted more, although they hadn't talked about it, and she just assumed he didn't.

She had been going to point out the tool chest along the walls and talk about where the keys were, but she had to think for a moment to remember and get her train of thought back.

Talking about machinery and equipment and tools and the farm in general was fun for her, and she enjoyed it. But...she also wanted to somehow fix their relationship or even maybe start their relationship, since they didn't really have one.

She wanted to get things settled—what his thoughts were and where he saw it going.

But sometimes, a person couldn't see the end from the beginning; sometimes, they couldn't even really see where the next step was. Sometimes, you just had to walk in the dark, having faith that things would work out and not demanding to know every step to get there before you agreed to put one foot in front of another.

"The keys for the tool chests are in the kitchen hanging on the key hook by the back door. I'll show you when we go in. That's pretty much where I have everything right now. Normally, we keep things unlocked and open, but since I knew I wasn't going to be using it and it was common knowledge around town that it would be here unattended, I wanted to keep things locked up."

"Prairie Rose doesn't exactly seem like a hotbed of crime."

"It's not. Although, there have been a lot of people moving in, people who don't necessarily fit with our way of life, and crime has increased. It's not as safe as it used to be."

She supposed every generation looked back on their childhood and thought they were better. So she didn't go any further down that rabbit trail.

They walked around the farm, discussing what her father had usually done, with Shawn throwing out ideas of his own. She would gladly go along with them, just happy to have someone else to talk to, to work with, to share everything with.

They talked about how some things that worked in Arkansas might not work in Iowa and about some things he wanted to try.

When it was time to pick up the girls, she went into town while he stayed, grabbing the keys and saying he was going to go out and make a list of the things that he wanted to do repairs on over the winter.

The ring on her finger felt heavy, but also right, as she walked away toward her car, feeling like it had been a simple day despite the huge changes that had taken place.

Somehow though, she felt it was like what Shawn had said.

God had provided a door, He'd opened it, and she'd walked through.

Maybe there really would be blessings on the other side.

Maybe it just showed how her life had gone, but it felt almost daring to hope that could be true.

Chapter 15

"I can help with the dishes," Shawn said as they got up from the table after supper that evening.

What Bridget had said earlier about this being the least romantic wedding day she'd had had kind of hit him. He hadn't thought about comparisons until that point.

Race had always been very clear that he could compete against himself, or he could keep his eyes on Jesus, but to look at other people was a joy killer.

He hadn't always appreciated his dad's wisdom, but that was one thing that he'd been pretty good at. He'd never really cared what everyone else was doing and never watched to see. Or to think about where he was in comparison to them. He just plowed his own path and walked on it.

But this...this husband thing.

Not even the husband thing as much as...the relationship thing.

Funny, but he wanted to be the best in Bridget's eyes. He wanted her to look at him and see a man better than other men. To feel like she'd gotten a good thing when he walked into her life. The best thing.

It had been a blow when she'd said that he was the least romantic, because up until that point, he hadn't even realized he wanted to be the best. All of a sudden, not only did he know he wanted to be the best, but he also knew that he was failing. Or had failed. He'd never have a chance to go back and do it again.

So, the very least he could do was to offer to do the dishes on her wedding day. Which had not been very special and not romantic at all.

What in the world did he know about romance?

"You worked hard today; this afternoon, you were even up at the chicken house when we got home from school. You take it easy, and I can grab the dishes. It's the least I can do to help."

"Well, maybe Elyse won't mind doing them with me?" He looked over at Bridget's second daughter, who was already gathering the plates up from the table.

"I can," she said, shrugging her thin shoulders.

She seemed to be the most easygoing of the three girls. All of them, while not responding with excitement, exactly, at his presence, had accepted him without any qualms, although Robin had given him a suspicious look or two. He thought that had to do more with the curse than with her not caring for him.

"If you're sure, I have some laundry I need to get out of the dryer. I'll go do that," Bridget said, meeting his eyes and waiting for his nod before she walked out of the room and into the side room off the kitchen that doubled as a mudroom and the laundry room.

"I heard you tell your mom you got a part in your school play at supper. Then we started talking about something else, and I didn't hear which part you had."

"I'm going to sing in the choir, and I'm going to be an angel. It's not the Mary and Joseph story from the Bible, but it's a play that has angels in it."

"Cool. I remember my sisters always wanted to play angels. In fact, I remember one of them came home crying from school one day when she didn't get the angel part that she wanted."

"That was me last year," Elyse said, setting the cups in the sink and walking back to the table to get the food.

"Really? That's sad. Did you change something in order to get chosen this year?"

"Mom said I had to go to the drama director and ask her what I needed to do in order to be better and get a part this year. That was last year. So, I didn't really want to do that because I was kinda scared. But my mom said if I really wanted it, I needed to work for it and not just complain that I didn't get it."

The little girl sounded so intelligent and matter-of-fact. He loved that Bridget had given her such great advice too. So many times, parents commiserated with their kids, saying so-and-so was a favorite, or the teacher wasn't being fair, or even just telling them to shrug it off and try again next year.

While those things might be true—teachers did have favorites, and sometimes the people that deserved the parts didn't get them—Bridget had actually given her daughter the responsibility and told her it was up to her to make her own future.

He wasn't even sure he would have thought to do that.

"And it paid off."

"It did. The part I got isn't very big, but it's better than the part I got last year, which was nothing."

"Then maybe if you work hard, learn your lines, do everything the teacher wants, and do a really good job on it this year, you'll get something more next year."

"Actually, I'm going to the teacher, and I'm going to ask her what I need to work on in order to get a better part next year. I mean, come on, it worked last year, right?"

"It did."

"Mom said I need to be careful not to take advantage of the teacher, though. She said the teacher has to have time for everyone and that I can't expect her to spend all of her time on me."

Shawn wrung out the rag and wiped the table that had been completely cleared. "Your teacher probably has a family as well. So teaching school and teaching drama isn't just what she does."

"Mom said that too. But she said it wouldn't hurt to ask. And she also said that if the teacher didn't have time or didn't want to work with me anymore, I could ask the teacher if she had any recommendations of where I should go."

"She might even give you acting lessons if you pay for them," Shawn said, taking the rag back over to the sink and rinsing it out.

"Mom said that too. But she said that we couldn't afford to pay if they were too expensive."

"I see." If Elyse wanted acting lessons, he thought they should try to make that work. But Bridget and he hadn't exactly sat down and talked about the farm's finances.

"You think you might want to be an actress when you grow up?" he asked, not sure how he felt about that. He didn't want to crush her dreams, but the chances of anyone becoming an actress were extremely low. It took more than just talent and hard work.

"No. I want to be a farmer. But being in the play is something I really like. It's fun. Like, a lot of my friends want to play basketball and run track. Not me." She gave an exaggerated shiver and stuck her tongue out, just in case he missed the implication that she hated sports. "But it's fun to dress up and basically play pretend. Although, it's a lot of work to memorize lines."

"Do you have many lines to memorize?"

"Just three." She put the glasses in the dishwasher and didn't look up.

"Are your sisters interested in acting?"

"Nope. All Robin wants to do is read. She even reads sometimes while she's packing eggs if Mom's not at the barn with us."

"That seems like a recipe for dropping them."

"Yeah. She makes me promise not to tell when she does it, because she breaks a lot more eggs, and Mom would deal with her if she knew."

Although he was tempted to smile, because it seemed like a little thing, he did make note of it. If Robin could get away with doing things behind her mom's back now when she was only twelve, it would probably just get worse as she got older.

But maybe she resented the load she had to carry since Bridget had probably been very busy with caring for her father and taking care of the farm. Maybe there had been too much responsibility placed on her young shoulders.

That would be something he would talk to Bridget about. He certainly wouldn't do anything on his own.

Before he and Elyse could continue their conversation, Bridget came out of the laundry room carrying a neatly folded blanket with what looked like sheets folded on top.

"I have the sheets and blanket for you. Both rooms upstairs that are empty have double beds in them. If you want to follow me, I can show you the two of them and you could pick which one you want."

She stood there with her brows raised and a carefully bland look on her face.

He had assumed they would share a room, even though he hadn't figured that the physical side of their relationship would be moving very quickly. Still, he just assumed they would set things up the way he expected them to go on throughout the decades, hopefully, of their marriage.

But they hadn't talked about it, and apparently her expectations were different than his.

"I'll follow you," he said as he looked around the kitchen. Elyse was closing the dishwasher door and starting it. And everything else was finished.

"All right. This way."

She'd taken him all around the farm today, but he hadn't been in any room in the house aside from the kitchen.

They didn't go through the dining room but went through a little hallway that led to a small landing where the stairs went up on one side and the dining room and living room opened up on either end.

Bridget was using both hands to carry the bedsheets, but she nodded her head toward the living room. "We don't use that room too often, but if we have a movie night or something, we go in there. Most of the time, we do schoolwork and stuff around the kitchen table and bigger projects around the dining room table. That's where we have company as well."

He nodded, studying her face, trying to figure out if there was some problem he had missed. She seemed a little more closed off than she had earlier.

Had the stress of the day gotten to her? Was she having second thoughts?

Or maybe she just wanted to make sure that he wasn't going to question her decree on the rooms.

He hadn't insisted on anything, going along with whatever she suggested.

This seemed like something he wanted to talk about.

So, when she pointed out the master bedroom and then walked on down the hall pointing to each of the girls' rooms, and the bathroom at the end of the hall, and the two rooms on either side of the bathroom that were unoccupied, he waited until she'd stopped before he said anything.

The shower was running in the bathroom, and he heard music coming out of one of the bedrooms. That took care of two girls. He wasn't sure exactly what Elyse was doing, but he figured this was as private as it was probably going to get.

"I thought we'd share a room," he finally said.

Her brows went up, but he thought it was less his comment that surprised her and more that he actually said it. Maybe she hadn't been expecting him to have an opinion of his own over it.

"How about we step into this room and we can talk about it in there," she said, nodding to the room to the left of the bathroom.

He pushed the door open and then waited for her to walk through, walking in behind her and closing it.

When she turned, she had the blankets squeezed tightly to her chest. His comment had upset her, made her nervous or scared.

He thought about waiting for her to talk, to give her side, or even just flat-out tell him he didn't know what he was talking about, but...watching her squeeze the blankets made him want to reassure her.

He wanted to touch her but kept his hands at his sides. "I'm not trying to say that anything needs to happen between us. But I assumed that's the kind of marriage we would have...eventually. I also assumed it would be better for the children to have us share a room from the get-go, rather than having the status of our relationship on display as it would be if I were living in a different room and eventually moved to yours." He assumed that's how that would work.

Regardless, she understood his point.

"I see. I hadn't thought about it that way. I'm not even sure the girls will really notice..."

"I'm sure they'll notice." He didn't know much about girls. Maybe even less about kids in general, but one thing he did know, not just from his own childhood, but from the counseling that his dad had done over the years with children, they were very much attuned to the relationship status of their parents. Very sensitive to the fights, disagreements, and anything that shook the stability of their world.

He didn't need a bunch of studies to prove that a traditional nuclear family was the best place for a child to grow up. In his experience, studies could prove anything they wanted to. Data could be manipulated to say anything.

But in his world experience, kids needed a solid relationship between their mom and their dad.

"You know, you're making me feel bad again."

"I'm sorry," he said immediately.

"No. I mean normally I think of my girls first in every decision that I make. This is the second time since yesterday that I've made a decision without considering their welfare." She shook her head, as though disgusted with herself.

"I fluster you. I think that's good. I'll take that." His words were light, and he allowed a smile to turn the corners of his mouth. He wanted her to not be so serious. They weren't talking about a life-or-death thing. Although he did have a definite preference, he wouldn't demand his way. Still, he was going to push for it a little harder than he had so far.

"I'm not sure I want you to know that." Her statement was not a denial, and that made his grin grow bigger. She took a look at it, and he didn't miss the tightening of her arms around the blankets and the slight tilt of her shoulder, almost as though she were angling herself just a little bit away from him for protection.

"I can pretend I didn't see a thing," he said, bending his head a little and trying to get her to meet his eyes again.

"I don't think I'm ready to share a room." Her words came out in a rush. "I understand what you're saying about the girls, and you're probably right, but...I'm just not ready to do that." She emphasized the word "that," and he understood that she wasn't talking about sharing a room.

For someone who had been married twice, she seemed a little skittish. But she hadn't been married long either time.

He stifled a sigh and calculated his words before he said, "I'm not pushing for anything more than the appearance of you and I being united by sharing a room. I just think that'll be good for the girls. Beyond that, if you want me to sleep on the floor, if you want me to sleep with coveralls on, if you want to put some kind of barrier down the middle of the bed, whatever makes you feel comfortable, I'm fine with it. The only thing I'm asking is that we start out as we mean to go on. And I mean to be sharing a room and having a relationship with my wife. That's how I want to go on. That's what I want to aim for. I promise I'll start out on a pallet on the floor in the far corner as far away from you as possible. But ultimately... Ultimately, I want a natural husband-wife relationship. But I'm willing to wait, and I'm willing to do that all on your timetable." He hoped he wasn't promising more than he could deliver there. If her timetable was thirty years on the floor, he wasn't sure he might not start pushing for a little bit of fast-forward, so he grunted. "Within reason. My reason being...a year?"

Her fingers were fisted in the blankets, and she looked like she'd swallowed a toad which had gotten stuck in her throat. Her teeth were gritted, but she nodded.

"A year. That sounds reasonable."

She seemed to have trouble getting her words out, but he waited. He wasn't going to push her.

"And I can be the one to sleep on the floor. I'm the one who doesn't want to move too quickly, so I should be the one to suffer."

"The someone sleeping on the floor will be me." He said that firmly, more firmly than he'd said anything, because he certainly wasn't going to be sleeping in the bed while his wife slept on the floor. That wasn't going to happen. Not ever.

"No. I don't want you sleeping on the floor."

"We can divide the bed. We can put pillows down the middle of it. We can rig up some kind of board to put down the middle of it if you want me to. But I'm not going to be sleeping on the bed while you sleep on the floor. And that's final."

So much for all the compromising and thinking about others that his dad had drilled into his head. He wasn't compromising on this point. Just wasn't.

Maybe she realized that, or maybe she didn't want to argue. She nodded her head. "I trust you. It's not that I don't trust you."

"Thank you. I appreciate knowing that." Because he was bigger and stronger than her, of course trust would be an issue. But she'd gotten his dad's recommendation, and she said herself that the way he'd acted had set her mind at ease. He didn't think she was necessarily scared of him in particular, just, like she said, not ready for more in their relationship. They'd barely talked to each other. They hadn't even shared a real kiss at their wedding. Of course she didn't feel comfortable with more.

"Okay," she said, seeming to force her hands to let go of the blankets. "I can still set these down here and make this bed. Maybe your parents would like to visit."

"I suppose they'll be around at some point," he said.

"We can share a bed." She nodded as though convincing herself of that point. "I have plenty of pillows. We can roll up a blanket. Just so I don't accidentally roll over on top of you in the middle of the night." Her smile was forced, but he acknowledged it with the quirk of his own lips.

"You don't need to put a divider into the bed for my sake. You rolling over on top of me isn't going to be a problem."

He'd rendered her speechless, and she turned her back on him, setting the blankets on the bed, straightening them out with much more show than necessary.

"Okay. Then I think we have that settled?"

"Are you good?" he asked, his words holding empathy and compassion. He had pushed her. He had demanded his way, and he wanted to make sure that he hadn't railroaded her into doing something she hated.

"Yes. Everything you said made sense. And I'm sure we'll be comfortable with each other very soon and this conversation will seem like it was completely unnecessary."

He wasn't so sure about that himself, but he let the comment go, nodding in agreement. "You could be right. Thank you. Thank you for giving me my way."

"Nobody's keeping score, but it's currently two to one," she said, lifting one of her brows before she reached past him and opened the door, walking out and leaving him with a bemused grin on his face.

Chapter 16

Three weeks later, they had settled into a routine. It was almost like Shawn had always been a part of their family.

In the summer, it would be a little different because he wouldn't be able to help in the chicken house every day if he was out in the fields. But for now, he helped both morning and evening, which took a lot of the load off of her shoulders and allowed her to cook breakfast, and it gave the girls another day off.

During the day, Shawn kept busy repairing equipment that had been sadly neglected.

After supper, they almost always spent some time as a family playing a game and reading a book together before bed.

As had been their custom before Shawn had joined the family, each girl had a different night to pick the game. And each girl took turns picking a new book.

While the girls didn't call Shawn "dad," they'd seemed to accept his presence in their home. After three weeks, they seemed completely comfortable with him.

"Portia, it's your turn to pick the game," Robin said once the dishes were cleaned up.

"Uno," Portia said immediately. But then she added, "And I want to do it under the table with a flashlight."

Bridget paused as she set her teacup in the sink. "Under the table?"

"Yeah. Like, you get the blankets that you get sometimes when we play house under the table. Only we'll play Uno under the table."

"It's going to be too dark to see, silly," Robin said with all the superiority of the oldest sister who was much bigger and much smarter than any of her annoying younger siblings.

"No, it won't. We'll use this!" Portia pulled the flashlight out from behind her back and shone it directly in Robin's eyes.

"Stop that!" Robin held out her hand and grabbed at the flashlight. "You're shining it in my eyes!"

"I know." Portia giggled.

"Portia, don't shine that in your sister's eyes."

"Robin, stop trying to hit your sister."

Bridget cringed, although that wasn't nearly the worst fight the girls'd had since Shawn joined their family.

He seemed to take their arguing in stride, unlike Blade who had been irritated to the point of anger when the girls fought.

But she'd learned that Shawn had five siblings, and she figured he was probably used to fighting. At the very least, he wasn't shocked to find out that her kids didn't always get along. That's the way Blade had acted. He'd been an only child, and rather sheltered, for all of his tough guy persona.

Her girls settled down, and Bridget did a quick debate in her head. Throwing blankets over the table and playing under it would add a little bit of work to game night, but it was special things like that that made sweet memories for her children. Maybe her kids wouldn't remember anything she did when they got older, but she had no memories of her mom, because her mom hadn't been there to make any, and she wanted to give her own children plenty of opportunities to make as many memories as they could.

"Do you mind?" she asked Shawn who sat at the table looking on his phone at the owner's manual of the big tractor, trying to figure out one of the wiring problems.

"Sure. I'm down for that. Can't say I've ever done it, to be honest."

"You've never played house under the table?" Portia asked, like that was something that everyone should have done at least once in their lifetime.

"Yeah, my sisters dragged me into that a lot. But we never played Uno with a flashlight under the table."

"Well, this is going to be Uno *and* house," Portia said in her bossy little girl voice. "You and Mom are the mom and dad, and Robin is the oldest sister, and Elyse is the second oldest sister, and I'm the baby."

"Okay." Shawn gave an exaggerated look of consternation. "I don't know if Robin's gonna be able to pull that off. That's going to take quite the acting skills there."

Robin rolled her eyes and grinned at Shawn. But she knew better than to argue with Portia, because if she didn't do what Portia wanted to do on her night, then her sisters would give her push-back whenever she wanted to do something that they didn't want to do on her night.

"Maybe Robin will take acting lessons with me," Elyse said, looking at Robin with an eager look like she thought it would be fun to have her sister taking acting lessons.

But Robin was a typical elder sister and rolled her eyes. "I'm not interested in acting lessons. Why would I want to do that?" She lifted her brows and gave her sisters a superior look before she turned to her mom. "Do you want me to get the blankets, Mom?"

"Sure," Bridget said, wondering if her girls would ever be best friends.

She'd always longed for a sister to have that special companionship with.

Maybe it was a thing of myth, since her girls didn't seem to share it.

"What can I do?" Shawn asked. "I've never done this before, so is there like a protocol to follow?"

"Not really. We'll move all the chairs back away from the dining table, and when Robin gets the blankets out here, we'll throw them over, turn out the lights, and crawl under." She looked at her youngest. "That's what you're thinking?"

"Yep," she said, flashing her light on and off.

Bridget had to grin at that. She remembered how much fun it was to play with flashlights when she was that age. It was even more fun when the lights were out.

Shawn moved the chairs back away from the table, and they had it set up in no time. He pulled the blanket back a little and said, "Do you want to go ahead and hop in before I turn the lights out?"

"Thanks," she said, ducking down and crawling in.

Elyse was already in, and Robin crawled in after her. Portia went in as well, and then the dining room lights went out.

"All right. I'm coming in, and I'll try not to step on anyone," Shawn said as he ducked in.

Bridget didn't have to hide her smile in the dark. She couldn't imagine either of her first two husbands humoring her children like this. Most of the time, Blade didn't participate in game night. Although Patrick had always been okay with reading to them.

It didn't make her first two husbands bad, or anything like that, it was just she loved that Shawn seemed to think that it was important for them to spend time as a family, and if that meant he was on the floor underneath the dining room table, he was willing to do it.

His hand landed on her leg. "Bridget?"

"Yep. That's my leg."

"I suppose the dad is supposed to sit beside the mom?" Shawn said, speaking into the darkness since Portia hadn't turned the light on yet.

"Yep. That's right. I can't find the flashlight though. You guys will have to wait a second. I think it rolled behind me."

Shawn chuckled softly, almost as though he, too, was remembering how much fun it was to play with a flashlight. Maybe he thought it was a little bit funny that he was feeling around in the dark trying not to step on anyone while he moved alongside of her and settled down with his side touching hers. His legs stretched out alongside hers, and his hand went behind her back, propping it on the floor as he leaned back slightly.

"Are you okay?" he asked softly.

"Things are a little bit tighter in here with another person."

"I'm bigger than you guys are too. Am I squishing you or anything?"

He was close. But she didn't feel squished. It felt cozy. In fact, she had to resist the urge to snuggle deeper into his arm.

She'd been feeling more and more comfortable with him, and she would certainly term their relationship "friends."

Not that she knew much about it, but she felt that was the best way to build a romantic relationship. On the foundation of friendship.

"I wish Shawn didn't have to die. I wish he could be our dad forever." Elyse's voice came out of the darkness beyond the rustling of Portia as she looked for her light.

Bridget gasped. "What are you talking about, Elyse?"

"She's talking about the curse. None of us can get too close to Mr. Shawn, because he's just going to die soon. But she's right. I don't remember my dad, but Mr. Shawn is much better than Mr. Blade. I wish he could stay forever." Robin sighed, her voice holding a little regret but also the confidence that came in dealing with facts.

"Yeah. I'm gonna talk to Caitlin at school tomorrow, but I'm pretty sure her dad doesn't get underneath the dining room table and play flashlight Uno with them."

Bridget supposed she should be thankful for small things, like the fact that her children hadn't said this before Shawn married her. If the townspeople couldn't change his mind, her children could if they kept talking like this. They weren't exactly a walking advertisement for her.

"I'm sorry," she said, her hand coming over and touching Shawn's leg to let him know she was talking to him. Then her voice got more strict. "Shawn isn't going anywhere. He's not dying." She wanted to believe it. Because she agreed with her girls. She wanted him to stay. She liked having him. And honestly, every day she got up and thought maybe this was the day that he would turn into something else, but so far, he was the same great guy that he'd been when they got married.

She was starting to think that was who he truly was.

"Are we supposed to just pretend it's not true?" Robin asked.

"No. No pretending. You act like it's not because it's not."

"But everyone says it is. They say Shawn's gonna die," Elyse added.

"Yeah. At recess, they take bets on how long they think he's gonna last. Some of them say their parents are doing the same thing," Robin added.

"I don't want him to die!" Portia wailed, her flashlight finally coming on with a click. "I don't want anyone to die! I want us all to be here together forever!" And then she burst into tears.

Bridget gritted her teeth. It was one thing for the townspeople to believe the curse. It was another thing for them to talk about it and allow their kids to go to school and say such terrible things.

She leaned over, holding her arms out to Portia, who found them and crawled into them.

"I've never wanted to strangle a little kid so much in my life. But I suppose all that anger should be directed at their parents," Shawn muttered. Then he blew out a long, slow breath.

"I think we ought to go over and throw eggs on their porch. That's what we can do with all our cracks. It wouldn't be wasting, because we throw some cracks away anyway," Robin said angrily.

Bridget's heart ached at the pain her children were suffering. Like losing two dads, an uncle, and their grandfather wasn't enough. They'd been through so much loss and pain. Did the town really have to make their lives that much worse by insisting that the man who'd married their mother and was quickly becoming an integral part of their family was going to die?

It made her breath come faster and her heart pump hard. If she were a violent person, she'd be dreaming up ways for those people to suffer for what they'd done to her girls.

"I think I have a better idea." Shawn shifted.

Chapter 17

"Bridget, you mind if we get out from under here for a second and go into the living room?" Shawn asked.

Bridget wanted to ask why, but she didn't need to know. He just asked if she minded. "No. We can do that," she said, biting her tongue over the "why" that wanted to come out at the end of the sentence anyway.

He leaned forward. "Hang on a second. I'll get out and turn the light on."

"But I want to play Uno!" Portia sobbed.

"And we will. But we have something we need to do first." Shawn's warmth disappeared from her side, and there was rustling as he moved the blanket and crawled out. Soon the light came on, and he peeled the blanket back so everyone could get out.

Elyse and Robin both had confused looks on their faces, but they filed out and walked slowly to the living room, neither one of them looking happy.

And why would they? If people at school were taking bets on when their stepdad was going to kick the bucket, that would upset anyone.

Shawn followed them into the living room. He pulled the coffee table away from the couch so that it was centered in the middle of the room.

"What are you doing?" Bridget couldn't stop herself from asking.

"I'm making an altar." He glanced up at her and then went back, picking up the two books and the coaster that were on the coffee table and moving them to the end table before coming back.

Bridget studied the coffee table, rolling his word over in her head. An altar?

It sounded... "If you're going to sacrifice one of my girls on this, I'm going to have to step in," she finally said just because she wasn't sure what else to say, and humor always seemed to defuse tense situations.

"You don't need to step in. But I am going to ask you guys to kneel," Shawn replied as he knelt himself at the coffee table.

That's what he meant by altar. An altar to pray at.

Of course. "Pray for those who use you and despitefully hurt and persecute you," she murmured as she knelt beside him, Portia on her other side.

She kept her arm around her daughter as the little girl lowered herself to her knees beside her mother.

Robin and Elyse followed suit, although their faces were a little confused. They'd never done anything like this as a family before.

"That's right. The family that prays together stays together."

"The effectual fervent prayer of a righteous man availeth much," she returned.

"Ask and it shall be given you; seek, and ye shall find; knock, and it shall be opened unto you."

"Call unto me and I will answer thee and shew thee great and mighty things which thou knowest not."

They laughed together. That was a competition she wouldn't mind engaging in. A Bible verse competition.

"I think Mom won," Robin declared.

"I guess I need to brush up on some more Bible verses to memorize, ha?" Shawn said with a glint in his eyes as he looked at Robin.

"Or maybe I'll memorize a bunch of Bible verses and beat you both," she said, her competitive streak from being the eldest coming out.

"I accept your challenge," Shawn said, lifting a brow in Robin's direction.

She loved that. Loved that he hadn't exactly tricked Robin into wanting to memorize Bible verses, but...he kinda had. At least he'd made her want to dig into the Bible. And once that happened, it would change her heart and her life. Whether she wanted it to or not. It was that powerful.

Bridget had to admit she was impressed. She was also grateful.

She turned her head and gave him a look, and as though he felt her eyes on him, he turned to meet her gaze.

His lips twitched just a little, acknowledging the fact that he knew exactly what he'd just done and was kind of happy about it himself.

She loved the little silent communication that was going on between them and making her feel like they were sharing a secret, just a warm and intimate feeling that served to pull her heart toward his.

She smiled but felt her cheeks heat at the same time, and she looked away as he began to speak.

"We just quoted the Bible verse that we're to pray for those who despitefully use us and persecute us. The Bible says we're supposed to return good for evil. We're supposed to turn the other cheek. That means when someone's unkind to us, we're supposed to return that unkindness with kindness." He had one knee bent on the floor, and his arm rested on his other. He looked at his hand before he lifted his head back up, looking around the table at the girls. "No one finds it natural to be nice to people who are being mean to them. No one finds it natural or easy to return good for evil. You have to work at it. You have to ask God to help you."

He breathed deep, as though needing to release his own irritation. "I thought that's what we should do. Ask God to help us and then follow the command. We'll pray for those who despitefully use us and persecute us. And then we're gonna look for ways to be nice to them. If we can."

"You said you wanted to throttle them."

"That's true. I do. You have no idea how angry it makes me to think of people talking about my family like that. Sending their kids to school and having their kids talk to my kids like that. It hurts. And I want to lash out in anger. That's what I was saying, that's the natural response."

"Yeah, I wanted to slap her little mouth," Robin muttered.

"Me too. But again, are we gonna do what we want to do? What we feel like doing? Or are we going to do what the Bible tells us to do? The Bible way is harder, but it puts us in a different category, not because we're better, but because we're different. God says that Christians should be different. This is one of the ways."

"I really don't feel like praying for anybody," Elyse said, very seriously.

"I'll be honest, neither do I. But the more you do it, the easier it gets. It's like acting. The more you practice, the more lessons you take and work at, the better you get. The more you practice being a good actress, the better you get at it. Same thing for being a Christian. The more you do what God tells you to do, even though it's hard, the more you practice being a good Christian, the easier it gets and the better you get at it."

"You understand?" Shawn asked Robin, tenderness in his tone.

She nodded, her chin going up and down and her shoulders relaxing a little. "It's like swimming. I wasn't very good at it, but I worked hard at it, and I got better. Now I can dive into the deep end of the pool and I can swim the whole way to the shallow end and back without stopping."

Shawn nodded. "That's exactly right. The more you practice being a Christian, the easier it is." He huffed a little. "But of course, you can't really know how to be a good Christian unless you know what the Bible says. Because the things we think are right aren't always what God says is right. And that's why it's a good idea to memorize it. Not just to win verse wars with your parents, but you can hardly know what God wants you to do if you don't know what the Bible says about what God wants you to do."

He was doing a great job. Being a dad while Bridget just sat there. So she added, "There's a lot of misinformation out in the world about what a Christian really should be."

Shawn nodded, then met her eyes before he bowed his head and all the girls followed suit.

Bridget listened as he prayed, her heart full. She'd felt him tense beside her. She'd heard his mumbled words. She knew that praying wasn't what he wanted to do. She also admired him for resisting what his flesh wanted to do and instead taking the opportunity to not just bring his own flesh under submission but to teach her daughters about it as well.

By the time he was done praying, she wanted to cry. Not out of sadness, but because of the deep appreciation and love in her heart that God had given her a righteous man, who was going to try with everything he had to make sure her daughters were brought up in the nurture and admonition of the Lord.

She cringed inside as she thought of how she'd actually sat on the back of her car, eaten watermelon with him, and argued with him about him wanting to have anything to do with her. Trying to drive him away.

Look at what she would have missed if she had been successful.

Look at what you would have missed if you hadn't gone through everything you did in order to get to where you are now. If you hadn't lost your husbands and brother, and if your dad hadn't been in the accident, and if he hadn't died, Shawn might not be here, and he certainly wouldn't have thought it important to marry you.

As the thought rolled through her head, she knew immediately it was right.

Sometimes, it took God's plan a really long time to roll out, but she couldn't say she was upset about the way it was looking. It seemed like God had worked all those other things in her life in order to give her something beautiful now.

She thought about the door that Shawn had told her would open, and she could walk through, and even though it seemed like a hard thing, she'd have blessings because of it.

Whether or not the curse was real, whether or not he stayed, she would remember this night for the rest of her life.

Chapter 18

The week after Thanksgiving, Shawn worked alone in the equipment shed, the tractor tire off, the tractor up on a jack, fixing an issue with the axle.

The glow from Thanksgiving was still fresh, and he looked forward to Christmas. His first Christmas with a family of his own.

It was kinda crazy how the girls already seemed to be like his, and, so help him, he was falling deeper in love with his wife every day.

He probably ought to tell her.

But she'd said a year, or at least that's what they'd agreed to from what he could remember of the conversation they'd had on their wedding day. He didn't want to rush her.

He was trying to think of what he could get her for Christmas. Something meaningful to let her know how he felt, even if it might be too soon for her to hear the words.

She wasn't a jewelry person, although he had caught her at various times admiring the engagement ring that had come back from being sized and that she wore along with her wedding band on her ring finger.

He'd caught himself admiring it too. Not the ring necessarily, but the hand.

It was a hardworking hand, tender and compassionate with her children, knowledgeable with the chickens. Skillful with the eggs, and it felt just right when her fingers slid between his, and they clasped together.

He couldn't think of too many other things he'd rather do than touch his wife. Holding hands gave him a connected feeling, a physical anchor, but more than that, a soul anchor, a feeling of belonging he couldn't remember ever experiencing before.

Race and Penny had raised him and he loved them, but...this just must be what God created him for. When a man and woman came together and created their own family. This almost supernatural feeling that he and his wife were one.

Silly thoughts for a man for sure.

He should be paying more attention to what he was doing on the tractor. He couldn't remember where he'd put his wrench down and felt around under the tractor for it while he lay on his back in the small space.

Maybe he hadn't been paying very good attention when he'd set the tractor up on the jack, or maybe it was just one of those things that was bound to happen at some point, but as he felt along on the ground for his wrench, his hand hit the block that he'd set the jack on. It must have been off balance somehow, because the block came out, the jack buckled under the weight, and the tractor came down on top of him.

Chapter 19

"So how's married life?" Miss Matilda asked, settling back in her chair, looking like she was eager for a little afternoon chat.

Bridget's cheeks warmed, and she looked down at her tea. Normally, Miss Matilda and her grandsons spent Thanksgiving together with her and her family.

They had this year as well, but they hadn't spent as much time talking as they normally did since there were so many people in Shawn's family.

She hadn't minded at all and in fact loved the loud craziness of celebrating a holiday with so many people.

But it did make having intimate conversations like this almost impossible.

"It's better than I ever dreamed," Bridget said honestly.

Miss Matilda nodded knowingly. "The third time's the charm," she said, then she sobered immediately. "That's just a phrase. Because I don't believe in charms, any more than I believe in curses. God gave you a good one this time."

"He sure did," Bridget said, meaning that with all of her heart. God had blessed her with an amazing man.

Her first two husbands were good men. But Shawn... Shawn was more than just a good man. Although he was that. He was an incredible father, a conscientious husband, a hardworking man, and there was so much for her to admire, so much for her to look at and feel blessed about, and he made her feel loved with the way he looked at her, the way he treated her...

"I think I'm falling in love with my husband," she said, looking out the window. It was about time for her to pick up her girls.

"Oh, I think you've already done that, honey. I think you were in love with him the first day you came here and told me about the man that you'd sat on the back of your car and eaten the watermelon with." Miss Matilda grunted a little. "That set him apart right there, from your first meeting."

"You're right. He was different from the beginning." She hadn't realized how different, and she meant "different" in the very best way.

Different as in an amazing, she didn't deserve him kind of way.

"It was nice of you to still have my grandsons and me over for Thanksgiving, even though his family was coming."

"You guys are like family to me, how could I not?" Bridget said, thinking about Braxton and how unhappy he had looked. Brooding and intense.

She'd almost said something to him after the meal, but she'd wanted to make a good impression on Shawn's family and hadn't wanted to leave them to entertain themselves while she sought out a man she wasn't married to, even if that man felt more like a brother than anything.

"Have you happened to talk to Braxton lately?" she asked, a little uncertainly because she probably should be asking Braxton himself and not his grandmother if there was a problem.

"No." Miss Matilda sighed. "But Elias was telling me that he's been short-tempered and grouchy. Although that's not the thing that concerns me the most."

"Oh?" Bridget asked, stirring her tea.

"Elias said Braxton was talking about moving."

"Off the farm?" Bridget asked, surprised. Although she supposed that Arian was growing older and maybe he wanted to be closer to the school so she could participate in extracurricular activities and wouldn't require such a long drive to and from the school property.

"Out of the state."

"He wants to leave Iowa?" Bridget exclaimed, her spoon clanking against her cup as tea spilled out over the rim. "Oh, I'm sorry." She grabbed a napkin and blotted up the liquid.

"No. That's exactly how I felt when I heard it. No one loves this land more fiercely than Braxton does. The farm, it's in his blood. He left for a while, because he was in love." Miss Matilda said that sweetly and almost dreamily. Underneath all of the good advice Miss Matilda always gave, she was a definite romantic. "But he came back. And vowed never to leave again. But...I think there's a problem."

"There has to be a problem if he's talking about leaving Iowa."

"With Arian's mother."

"Oh," Bridget said and bunched her lips up tight. She was tempted to say that Braxton was still in love with her. Even though Braxton hadn't sworn her to secrecy, she wouldn't give away anything he might not want everyone to know. Not even his grandmother.

But it turned out she didn't have to.

"I know he still loves Arian's mother." Miss Matilda sighed again. "I know there are good reasons for them not to be together, although I don't know what they are."

Her words were almost apologetic, and Bridget shrugged her shoulders. She didn't know either.

"I just know the little girl would love to have a mother. I don't even know if she knows who she is." She seemed to force a smile on her face. "But, if life were perfect, it would be boring, and what would be the point anyway?"

Bridget nodded, agreeing and, for the first time in her life, really feeling it. If she hadn't gone through the trials that she had gone through earlier in her life, she probably wouldn't appreciate the man who had married her now.

"Next week when I come, maybe we can get your tree out," Bridget finally said after a little more silence. There wasn't any point talking about Braxton anymore. She couldn't help him, and it sounded like he wasn't willing to help himself.

"That'll be fun. I have to make sure I'm stocked up on hot chocolate when I order my groceries next week."

"We might have to do it after school so the girls can help. When you say hot chocolate, they'll pretty much do anything."

"They're good girls. You have a wonderful family." Miss Matilda smiled and slowly stood.

Bridget gave her a hug, said a few more words, and hurried out. She was just a little late picking up the girls, and she didn't want them to have to wait in front of the school for her.

When she got home, she'd have to talk to Shawn about putting their own tree up. The girls and she always had fun driving along the fence with her dad, picking out the perfect tree. Last year had been a little different because she'd been taking care of her father, and they'd just had a small tree, one she could easily cut down.

Hopefully, Shawn would be willing to go out and do their tree tradition with them.

Bridget laughed at herself. There hadn't been anything he hadn't been willing to do. Other than not share a room with her. She kinda felt like he was fighting for her rather than against her with that one anyway.

She drove to the school with a smile on her face.

Chapter 20

Bridget hummed softly to herself as she walked into the egg house, carefully stepping on the mat and changing her shoes.

She wasn't too surprised that Shawn wasn't standing at the egg belt packing eggs. He probably hadn't made it the whole way around picking up floor eggs.

Usually, he was right on time and had things well in hand until she got there with whichever girl's turn it was, but a couple of times, he'd been a little later, explaining he'd been in the middle of a project and hadn't wanted to quit until it was done.

She assumed that's what had happened today and why he wasn't there. She didn't mind. Not at all.

She'd never even asked him to help; he'd just done it.

She certainly appreciated it, but she didn't want to get to the point where she expected it from him if he had something else that was more important or that he'd rather do.

But then, as she walked out of the control room, her eyes landed on the blue basket. It was empty. He hadn't even made it up to the barn yet.

Goodness, he'd never been this late. He must be really involved in something. Sometimes in the evening, he talked about the equipment that he was fixing, and she paid attention, truly she did, but she could not always tell which tractor was which, and when he talked about replacing a driveline or welding a cracked cutter bar, she didn't always know exactly what he was talking about.

They'd laughed about it several times when she'd said something like, "I hear you, and I can repeat what you said, but I have no idea what you're talking about."

He didn't take umbrage, and he patiently answered any questions she had while recognizing the fact that she would never be as interested in it as he was.

But it was part of life on the farm, and she didn't mind at all hearing about it.

Who knew? Maybe someday she'd actually learn something and be able to fix something herself.

"I'm getting the basket and going to pick up floor eggs," Bridget said to Robin as Robin finished changing her shoes and stepped into the packing room.

"Okay. I'll start doing the eggs."

Bridget's phone buzzed with a text, and she pulled it out as she walked over to the basket.

It was Penny, Shawn's mom.

I was hoping we could get some plans nailed down for Christmas. I know you guys can't leave the farm, on account of having to do the eggs. A couple of Shawn's siblings are going to their in-laws for Christmas Day. Could we find a day that would work for everyone to come to Iowa and celebrate Christmas?

She stared at her phone, her throat backing up. Penny had gone out of her way to make her feel included and had never, not even one time, mentioned that she might not be as much a part of the family as everyone else was, just because Shawn and she hadn't exactly been a love match.

The words "marriage of convenience" hadn't even been uttered.

Of course, as she thought about it, she didn't think Shawn had ever really believed that their marriage would just be convenience.

From the very first, he'd wanted a real marriage; they'd just gotten married before he began to court her. That's what it felt like. That he was courting her.

She stood beside the basket while her thumbs flew over her phone.

Absolutely! We'll make whatever day works for everyone else work for us too. It's so kind of you to come here, since you know we can't leave. I've already talked to Shawn about going down to visit all of you when this flock of birds goes out and we have a couple of weeks off.

She shoved her phone in her pocket and walked out, surprised at the little worry in the back of her mind.

Where was he?

The worry twisted and poked, making her glance around, wishing Shawn were there.

Just because he'd never missed an evening packing eggs didn't mean he wouldn't. So he got caught up in something. It was okay.

By the time she got to the other end of the barn, the basket was heavy and so was her heart.

From now on, she was going to make it a practice to go see her husband before she started the barn work. Not because she necessarily needed him to help her with it, but just because she wanted to put eyes on him, make sure he was okay. The heaviness of the little tingle of worry in the back of her mind had become a brick wall, and it weighed down heavy.

It was perfectly natural for a wife to want to talk to her husband. He wouldn't read anything extra into it. It wouldn't be a telltale sign that she'd fallen in love with him.

And what would it matter if he knew anyhow?

Except, if he didn't return her feelings, that could make everything awkward. And they'd fallen into such a nice routine. She didn't want everything to be awkward when things had just started to feel so natural and right.

Except...she wanted more. It wasn't completely natural for husband and wife to just be friends. They were supposed to be more.

She wasn't sure that was a conversation she knew how to start, though.

The worry hadn't gotten any better when she walked through the door with a full basket of eggs. She set them on the sink and started to wash them, trying to think about something other than the fact that her husband wasn't there, when Robin said from behind her, "Do you think we can get Mr. Shawn to take us for a Christmas tree like Pap used to?"

"I'm sure he will," Bridget said with confidence. There wasn't anything that they'd asked him to do that he hadn't done if he was able. Although cutting a tree down could be a little bit dangerous.

Not that they ever cut any trees that were big enough to hurt anyone, but just using a chainsaw... Maybe she didn't want him to do that. He'd almost convinced her that the curse was bogus, but still, she didn't want him taking any chances.

"I think I know where there's a good one. I was watching this summer when we drove back along the fields, and I think I can find it and show it to you."

"Well, you know the deal. Everyone has to agree."

Sometimes, that took a really long time, but it made it fun too.

"I know." Robin giggled. "Going for the Christmas tree is my favorite part of Christmas. I can't believe it's almost here!"

"It's one of my favorite parts too. Although I like decorating it as well," Bridget said, grateful for a conversation that helped take her mind off the clenching of her stomach.

Unconsciously, her ears were straining to hear the outside door open, to hear footsteps, to hear Shawn's voice.

"Don't you think it's odd that he's not here yet?" Robin said after she talked about how much she liked their tree last year and how she wanted to decorate their tree this year exactly the same way.

Bridget realized she'd been clenching her jaw, a manifestation of the nervousness she was feeling.

Robin was going to think it terrible, because she couldn't remember ever leaving the packing room before the work was done in the evening.

They just didn't quit and run anywhere, but she finally said, "Will you be okay here for a few minutes? I just remembered something I wanted to ask Mr. Shawn."

She grabbed the towel and turned to look at her daughter while she dried her hands. As she figured, Robin's face registered surprise, but it also showed relief.

"Go ahead. I've kind of been a little worried. You don't think anything happened to him?"

That dreaded curse. She should have known. Probably the second they stepped in the packing room and Robin had seen he wasn't there, she'd started worrying. Bridget should have gone immediately to check on him.

"I'm sure he's fine," she said, summoning up a reassuring smile, when she felt anything but.

"Okay." Robin didn't sound sure at all. "What do you have to ask him?"

"It's just one of those things that I can't tell you, or I'd have to sew your lips shut." Bridget tried to wink and sound like she was teasing.

That's what she'd say sometimes when she was hiding birthday presents or Christmas presents or planning a surprise party.

It worked, and Robin grinned, the wheels of her mind already working to try to figure out what secret her mom might be keeping from her.

It showed how upset she was, but Bridget didn't even bother to change out of her egg room shoes and into her regular shoes when she walked out. She did manage to walk sedately to the door and not start a full-out sprint until she was out of Robin's sight.

She was out of breath when she made it to the machine shed. That would be the first place she looked. If he wasn't there, she'd go around to several of the other buildings before she started to really panic.

Yanking the door open, her panic eased just a little when she saw the lights were on. That probably meant he was in here.

But there wasn't any noise. No clanging, no banging, no sound of a motor, a drill, a grinder, the welder. Nothing. It was way, way too quiet.

That's when she saw his legs sticking out from underneath the tractor, the front axle of the tractor lying on top of one of them.

Nearby was the knocked-over jack and the block he'd probably used to set the jack on since they didn't have any jacks that were big enough to hold the tractor up.

She'd remembered her dad talking about that.

Her heart had jumped painfully into her throat, and her stomach twisted, drawing her ribs in tightly. She wanted to double over from the pain in her abdomen.

She also didn't want to walk forward. If Shawn were dead, she didn't want that sight to be the last memory she had of him. Whatever his mangled body looked like underneath the tractor.

"Shawn?" she said, her voice a thready, pathetic sound in the cavernous interior of the machine shed.

"Bridget!" His voice, weak, seeming like it was dragged out of the depths of his chest, was the best thing she'd heard in decades. She stopped her slow tiptoe and rushed over to the side of the tractor. Scared of what she was going to see but now desperate to get him out.

She'd dug her phone out of her pocket when he said, "Get the jack and get the tractor off of me."

Those words weren't any stronger than his earlier one, but her eyes ran over him, and the only thing she could see was the tractor's axle sitting on his leg. It was heavy and pinned him down, and he couldn't move, but it was propped in such a way that the underside of the gearbox had missed his chest and lay almost on the ground beside him. There was just enough room for the width of his body between the two pieces that had landed on the floor.

But barely any room for his chest to rise and fall. He was slowly suffocating.

"Let me call an ambulance first."

"Get it off me. Use the jack." He'd never used that tone with her before. Even though his voice still wasn't strong, she didn't argue, but dropped her phone immediately, and grabbed the jack. She didn't bother with the hunk of wood. She only needed to get it a couple of inches up to get his leg out, and it just needed to hold a few seconds for him to slide out.

She didn't know how to fix anything, couldn't even begin to start to think of how to fix things, but she did know how to work a jack. She slid it under, close to his leg, at a point that would hold the weight, and absentmindedly noted that there was no blood on the floor.

Picking it off of him might release the pressure and start him bleeding though. She was probably going to have to deal with him going into shock.

She had no idea how to do that.

She wished he would have allowed her to call an ambulance, but he was probably right. The most important thing was to get the tractor off.

"Do you know what to do about shock?" she asked as she grabbed the bar, put it on the jack's handle, and started pumping.

"You can Google it while you drive me to the hospital." His words came out puffy and weak. "Better yet, I'll Google it. You drive."

"At least you're letting me take you to the hospital," she said, not a little bit of sarcasm in her voice, although this really wasn't the time. Still, if he were any more hardheaded, he would probably insist that he didn't need to go.

"That's a good point. I don't think I need to go."

"You are going," she said in a voice that she had never used before. Not even on her children.

"I think she cares about me," he said, laughter in his voice, despite the lack of volume and strength.

"I am not going to laugh at any of your jokes. Don't even."

"This is the best time. You can't let an accident go by without wringing all the humor you can out of it."

"Oh yes, we can. We are serious, and we are going to get you out of here and into the hospital, and we will laugh when you are better." She was still using that same tone. That bossy, commanding, you are not going to argue with me or I'm going to hit you over the head with this handle extension tone of voice.

"You're going to argue with the man when he's down?"

"I think that's the only way I'm going to win an argument with you."

"It's two to one," he reminded her.

"That's only because we haven't been keeping track, because you said you don't keep count. But I'm winning, and you owe me. So shut up and roll." She ended the last kind of loud, since she just got the tractor up far enough that he could get out, and she wasn't going to be able to breathe until he was out. Then if the tractor wanted to fall to pieces, it could.

"Give me your hand. Pull me."

His voice sounded a little better, and that's when she realized that part of the tractor actually had been sitting on his chest. Not hard enough to crush it, but enough that he hadn't been able to breathe.

"My ribs are a little sore."

"They're probably broken," she muttered, grabbing his hand, then realizing it was really going to hurt him as she pulled.

He grunted but moved with her as she pulled on his hand. His body slid out from underneath the tractor easy enough on the cement floor.

"Help me up," he said, sounding a little better.

"How are you feeling?" she asked, moving to scrunch underneath his armpit so he could put his arm around her but looking him over, concerned.

As she had feared, his leg had started to bleed. The blood dripped down, soaking through his jeans.

"Like a tractor fell on me." His lips didn't smile, but his eyes twinkled.

"I told you no jokes," she said, her eyes wide, and she could only imagine how wild her face looked. It was only because of concern and fear that he could die.

"No fear," Shawn said.

"You'd better not die."

"If I do, you know you'll see me again. No fear."

"Stop it. I'm not going to listen to reason. You are going to listen to me. And you are not going to die."

By that time, he'd gotten to his feet, groaning just a little.

"Can you walk?"

"I can hop," Shawn said, grimacing. "But it's going to hurt."

"I should have brought the car around before I got you up. I'm afraid you'll pass out if I leave you here."

"Help me over to the stool. I'll sit there and wait for you. I'll Google shock while I'm waiting."

"Okay." She pushed her body against his and tried to take as much of his weight as she could as he took each painful hop.

"I suppose this isn't a good time to ask if I can kiss you," he said, sinking onto the stool and leaning his head back on the toolbox, his eyes closed.

"No. It's a terrible time."

"If I die, I'm gonna regret that."

She froze. "Wow. You are really milking this out."

"She's going to turn down what could possibly be my last request," he said, cracking one eye open and tilting his head at her.

"I don't think I've ever been this angry at someone before in my life," she said, her voice trembling, and she wasn't even sure why she was so angry.

"If you give me the silent treatment, does that mean no kissing?"

This time, both of his eyes were open, and his lips turned up a little bit. It was just a shadow of that smile that he always gave her, the one she couldn't resist returning. And somehow, the smile melted her anger, though not her intense fear, but it made her step closer and put her hand on his cheek.

"If I kiss you, will you promise that you won't die?" It was a promise he couldn't make. Couldn't keep, didn't have any control over, but it was what she wanted.

"That's a steep price. You want me to make a promise I can't guarantee I'll keep in order to get the one thing I want?"

She shook her head, her own smile somehow, someway, wanting to break open.

She lowered her head and brushed his lips with hers.

"Now you can die happy," she said.

If he was going to laugh about this, she was determined she would too. And if he really didn't make it, she didn't want to regret ruining their last minutes together with anger and fear.

"That's my girl," he said, his eyes closed again, his lips smiling. "If I promise to sit at the gate and wait for you, will you give me another one?"

She laughed. "Don't sit at the gate. Go in and enjoy it. You can give me the tour when I get there."

Now his eyes cracked, and his teeth emerged. "Man, I love your spunk."

"I love you," she whispered, lowering her head for the second kiss he'd requested, although somewhere in the back of her head, she was wondering what kind of responsible adult she was when she was kissing her husband instead of taking him to the hospital.

"Now I can't die," he said as she lifted her head.

"I already told you that," she whispered, her fingers trembling, her heart thumping loud and heavy.

"I want to look forward to a lifetime of that." His hand came up and brushed her cheek, then wrapped around her neck. "I guess I'll have to listen to you this time."

"That's a relief," she whispered.

"You should have warned me before I married you what a devastatingly good kisser you are."

"I wouldn't have wanted to ruin the surprise," she said and laughed when his eyes opened. "You stay there. I'm going to grab the car."

"Hand me my phone, please. It's on that other tool chest."

She grabbed his phone and set it in his hand. "Google how to treat shock, just in case we need it. I'll be right back."

She ran to the car, calling Robin on the way. Breathlessly, she told her that she had to leave for a bit with Shawn and that Robin needed to shut the belt off and go to the house to watch her sisters.

She didn't say anything more, other than to tell Robin that she would explain everything when they came back, but it might be a couple of hours. She'd call her later when she knew more.

By that time, she'd stopped the car right beside the door, with enough space to open the passenger door, so that all Shawn had to do was walk in.

It was a little easier than what she thought, and it didn't take long for him to hop the distance between the stool where he sat and her car.

Until tonight, she had started to believe that the curse really was nothing. He'd convinced her, convinced her that he was going to live, that the townspeople would change their minds, that they'd believe them.

But now? Now it was obvious that it was just a matter of time, and she was gonna lose her husband. And it was going to hurt, the worst of any of them. She wasn't sure she'd survive.

Chapter 21

"A re you sure you want to come in with me? It will just be a minute to give her this bag of sugar."

Bridget didn't want to fuss over Shawn, but she was still a little worried about him. The ER doctor had done some X-rays, declared him fine, stitched his leg up, and told him to do a better job jacking up his tractor next time.

Now, a few stressful hours later, they were on their way home, but she had to stop in at Miss Matilda's and give her the bag of sugar they'd picked up at the grocery store.

"I'm sure," Shawn grunted as he pulled himself out of the car.

It was going to be tough to get the guy to take it easy, which is what the doctor had said, with a bit of a smirk, that Shawn needed to do. The smirk was probably because he knew that Shawn was the type of man who wasn't going to sit around and not do anything. He didn't have a take-it-easy bone in his body.

"If you have a message for Miss Matilda, I can tell her, and you can just sit there like the doctor told you to," Bridget said, trying to not sound irritated, although she knew she was hovering.

Any irritation was just left over from the fear she felt when she'd seen him under the tractor.

They hadn't needed the instructions to treat shock, not for him. She definitely felt like she could crash. It could be her that would need to be treated for shock.

"I just want to see her. I've met her at church a couple times, but I've never been in her house."

That sounded like an excuse to Bridget. Shawn just didn't want to sit around in the car.

She could call him on it, or she could just go along.

Normally it wouldn't even be a question, but she would really prefer that he took it easy.

She hadn't been joking when she said she'd fallen in love with him. She didn't want him to succumb to the curse.

Still, she didn't want to spend whatever time she did have with him fighting. So she closed her mouth and led the way to Miss Matilda's back door.

Bridget opened the door after knocking and called out like she usually did before she stood back, but Shawn wouldn't go first. He shook his head, his lips lifted.

"I'm not old and decrepit yet. Ladies first."

She rolled her eyes and then breezed in the house, thankful that he hadn't thought to yank the sugar from her. She went straight to the cupboard and put the sugar away.

By the time she turned around, Miss Matilda was in the doorway.

"Both of you? What a pleasure," the lady said.

"Both of us, because Shawn's been at the ER, and I stopped on the way home to grab your sugar."

"My goodness, I appreciate it, since I want to make those pies first thing in the morning, but you didn't need to do that." She stopped and her eyes grew big. "Emergency room?" She walked in a little further and looked Shawn up and down.

He grinned. "A tractor fell on me. I survived. I think that proves the curse is a bust." His grin grew bigger, and Bridget shook her head at his cockiness. "That just means the curse is real. And it didn't work. So it will be coming after you again!" She definitely had more feeling in those words than she meant to show. More fear. More exasperation. More not wanting him to taunt death, because death could get him next time.

Miss Matilda shook her head. Smiling. "Bridget. You don't want him to be any different than what he is."

"No. You're right. He's alive right now, and I don't want him dead," she said, irritation lacing her words, although she didn't mean it to.

"Tell her the curse isn't real," Shawn said, limping over, and putting a hand on Bridget's shoulder.

She wanted to jerk away. She was angry enough to do that, or emotional enough, but that wasn't the kind of relationship she wanted to have.

She didn't want her husband to worry about whether or not he could touch her, or whether she was going to jerk away and not let him, to give up touching her altogether because he didn't know how she was going to react.

So she turned her head up and allowed him to see the pleading in her eyes. Then she moved closer, putting her arm around him.

Whether or not he saw the pleading, she wasn't sure, but she saw their kiss reflected back in his, and her cheeks grew warm.

"I don't have any intentions of leaving you," he said softly. "But we have to live."

She knew it. And there was no safety on the farm. Every day brought danger. Not danger like a war zone, but danger like an accident could happen at any time. No one knew that better than she did.

"Accidents happen, Bridget," Miss Matilda said, coming over and standing between them, balancing herself with her hand on the back of one of the kitchen chairs.

"I want them to be accidents, then," she said. "And not attributed to the curse."

"You might never get rid of the curse. It might be something that you live with all of your life. You know, the way people have nicknames...maybe someone is called Buzz because of a buzz haircut, and they're eighty years old, and had one buzz haircut in their life, and their nickname is still Buzz. That's just life."

"But it's upsetting. My kids are upset. I'm upset. I don't want to hear people speculating and betting on when my husband is going to die."

"You know, I thought I would be able to crush the curse and prove that it wasn't true."

"Are you trying to tell me that you had the tractor fall on you on purpose?" Bridget asked, hand coming up on her hip, and she didn't care what kind of marriage she wanted or hoped to have. If he lay under a tractor and had it fall down on top of him on purpose, she was going to yank herself away and never talk to him again.

Ever.

"You know, I never thought of that. That probably would've been a good idea," he said, but she was pretty sure he was joking. "But still, there's going to be people that say exactly what you just said, which is, the curse didn't work this time, it'll get you next. I don't think it matters how many times I cheat death, how many times something could have killed me and doesn't, it doesn't matter how long I live, there are some people who are never going to let it go."

"He's right." Miss Matilda shook her head slowly. "A reputation is really hard to shake, even if it isn't deserved."

"I'm sorry. I know I told you that I was going to prove that it wasn't true, but as I rolled it over in my mind, trying to come up with a plan, there just isn't any. There's no way that the town isn't going to think for a really long time that there is a curse on the farm."

"I see," she said softly.

"I guess the thing that matters to me is, us. We don't believe in the curse. We believe in God, and His providence, His will, His protection. The Bible says safety is of the Lord, and we claim to believe the Bible, right?"

"He's right, Bridget," Miss Matilda said. "The Bible does say safety is of the Lord."

"I know. I believe it. At least, in theory. I can try to believe," she finally said.

"And our kids. We want our girls to know that sometimes people get crazy ideas in their heads, sometimes they do things that don't make any sense, and sometimes they do things that hurt us. But they can't make us change our minds, change what we believe, move our feet from the solid rock on which we stand and put a toe in the quicksand that's all around us. We'll just keep standing on the rock. We'll keep our girls beside us. And we'll live until God calls us home."

"That's better than a sermon on Sunday," Miss Matilda said.

Bridget snorted. "I hope that was the entire sermon and not just the first point. If he whips out a twenty-seven-point outline, I might have to go home by myself."

Shawn shook his head, grinning. "I'm no preacher. That's not what God made me for. But I do think...I do think He made me for you. I'm looking forward to the next five or six decades."

"He's romantic and a preacher." Miss Matilda put a hand over her heart. "I think some of my grandsons could take some lessons from him."

"No one who knows me back home in Arkansas would call me romantic. I think a man needs to find the right girl to bring the romance out in him."

"Bridget's the right girl for you, that's for sure."

As Bridget looked up into his eyes, and he smiled down at her, she thought maybe he was right. About everything.

Chapter 22

"This is the tree I want!" Robin said as she reached over Bridget and pointed out the cab of their enclosed ATV.

Robin sat between Shawn, who drove, and Bridget, who sat on the passenger side.

Elyse and Portia were in the back. They'd already pointed out their trees.

"What do you guys think?" Bridget asked.

"I think mine's better," Portia said.

"Yours is too big." Robin sounded reasonable. "Mine's a little bit too tall, but once Mr. Shawn cuts it down, it'll fit in the house just fine. And it's perfect. Look." She pointed over Bridget again. "There aren't any holes at all in it."

"But holes are what makes it fun!" Elyse exclaimed. "That's where we put all the pretty ornaments. Plus, that's the idea of a Christmas tree. We take one that looks kind of ugly and a little bit sad, and we decorate it and make it look beautiful. What's the point of taking one that already looks perfect?"

Bridget couldn't argue with that logic. In fact, it sounded like something she might have said last year. She probably had ulterior motives then, since she was the one responsible for cutting it down, and she wanted one that wasn't going to be too big or too heavy and also one that wasn't too hard to get to.

Still, it made sense.

"Mr. Shawn?" Robin asked, turning her head and looking at Shawn who sat looking at the tree with his hand on the wheel.

"This kind of feels like something that could get a little hot and contentious. I think we ought to put three numbers in a hat and pick out a number, and whoever's number wins, gets to pick the tree."

"We've never done it that way before," Bridget said. There was logic in that, and hopefully everyone would be happy with the result, since it was completely random.

The girls agreed, so Shawn pulled out a scrap of paper from his wallet, Bridget grabbed the pen from the side of the door, and they borrowed Portia's hat. Elyse ended up the winner, which made Bridget happy–they'd use a not-so-perfect tree for their Christmas tree this year. Fitting, since their lives had been not so perfect this year as well.

She liked the idea of taking something that wasn't perfect and using it anyway. Making it look pretty. Something the whole family would enjoy and admire.

The rest of the evening was busy, as they brought the tree home, got it set up, and decorated it. It was late when they sent the kids to bed.

And then...

"Are you ready?" Bridget asked.

"I am. Are you ready?" Shawn replied, his eyes twinkling.

They both knew that she was the one who needed to be sure, who needed to suck up her courage and take the plunge.

"I think. Are you going to be upset with me if I say no?"

"No. I've waited this long. I can wait another day or two."

"I'm sorry. I did make you wait longer than I should have."

"I don't want you to do it if you're not ready. I definitely don't want to push you into doing anything that's going to make you uncomfortable. This has to be something that we're both okay with."

"I'm pretty sure you're okay with it," she said, lowering her head and looking at him from underneath her lashes.

"I was pretty obvious about it?" he said.

"Yeah." She drew the word out a little. "You've kind of been bugging me about it for the last couple of days."

"Bugging? That doesn't sound very good. Are you sure that's the word you want to use?"

She pretended to think about it for a minute, and then she nodded. "Yep. Bugging is the best word."

"It's a good thing I'm not sensitive like some men are. You could really crush my ego."

"I'm not sure that's possible," she said, going to the counter where she had the fingernail clippers sitting in a small amount of alcohol.

"Oh, trust me. It's possible. Men look tough, but we've got very fragile egos."

"I know. And you're right. Bugging isn't the right word."

She picked up the fingernail clippers and walked back over to him. It had become natural to hold his hand, or to hug him, and even to reach up and press her lips to his.

She did that now. Just a short kiss, before she pulled away.

"Ready?"

"If your intention was to distract me from the imminent pain by kissing me, making me think of other things, it's working."

"All right. Go ahead and sit down on the couch, and I'll see if I can't distract you again before I get started."

"With an offer like that, I can't refuse."

She stepped back, her hands slid down his arm, their fingers clasping, as she led the way to the living room where he sat down on the couch.

She turned all the lights in the room on, making sure it was bright enough for her to see, before she pulled up the cuff of his jeans and exposed the wound that had been stitched up.

Taking a deep breath, she said, "And you're saying that your family does this all the time?"

"Sure. I mean, my dad's a surgeon, so, you know, he had professional training. But us boys have done it to each other. We can't go to the ER every time we have to have stitches taken out."

She still wasn't sure about it, but she said, "All right. I'll take your word for it."

"I can Facetime my dad if you need me to."

"No. I can do this. I've got a feeling I'm going to have to do it a lot anyway, so I might as well jump in and get started."

She knelt at his feet and met his eyes before she put his foot in her lap and pulled at the end of one string that was attached to the lowest knot.

"Does that hurt?"

"A little. Pinches, but that's to be expected. If you just move it back-and-forth, it will pull away from the skin, and loosen up. Then, just pull it up a little, clip one side, and it should slip right out."

She blew out a breath, and Shawn chuckled. "Just be thankful it's not staples. Those are a little trickier. A lot more painful."

"I'm guessing you have some scars from that," she said, muttering under her breath.

"Someday you'll see them," he said easily.

Her hand stilled, two fingers gripping one of the strings, the fingernail clippers hovering over the end that she was getting ready to snip. She looked up at him and said softly, "How about tonight?"

The easy grin faded from his face, and his chest froze.

Something darkened his eyes, and she was pretty sure that was a touch of eagerness lifting the corners.

"Are you sure?"

She nodded slowly. She'd been sure for a while, just not sure how to approach the subject with him, since Shawn seemed to be willing to wait for the entire year that they had talked about.

That year was looking longer and longer to her, and she found that curse or no curse, she wanted to seize the moment.

"I am."

"Maybe we can do the stitches tomorrow," he said, humor lurking back in his eyes.

"Are you afraid I'm gonna cause more harm than good getting the stitches out?"

"Maybe I don't want to take any chances."

"Chances of me hurting you, or chances of me changing my mind?"

"Both. Mostly the second."

"Will it put your mind at ease if I say my mind's been made up since the night you went to the ER? I just haven't figured out how to say anything until just now?"

"I still think the stitches can wait," he murmured.

"Lean back and close your eyes. These bad boys are coming out." She grinned at him, then lowered her head. Somehow taking the stitches out didn't seem nearly as difficult; in fact she couldn't wait to get it accomplished.

"Here we go," she said, and then snipped.

Chapter 23

S hawn held Bridget's hand as they strolled out of the school auditorium.

The Prairie Rose school Christmas program had made for a wonderful evening.

Actually, what made the evening wonderful was the fact that he'd gotten to spend it with his family. Satisfaction and contentment swelled in his chest as the girls chattered about their parts and Bridget smiled and nodded and occasionally offered a small comment, her hand tucked trustingly in his.

"I thought we'd walk out Main Street and grab some hot chocolate from the coffee shop beside the laundry mat if you ladies are up for it," he said as they exited the front doors of the school building, jostled some by the crowd.

"Yay!" Portia said. "Can we have hot chocolate, Mom?" She was practically jumping up and down and probably didn't need the extra sugar and caffeine, still going strong on the excitement of being on stage.

"If that's what Mr. Shawn wants to do," Bridget said easily.

"Daddy," Elise said firmly, slipping her hand into his, making his heart stop. His throat closed and his eyes burned. "Is it okay if I call you Daddy?" she asked, looking up, her brows drawn, like she was worried she might have done something wrong.

"There isn't too much that would make me happier," he said, managing to get the words out without his voice cracking, meeting Elise's eyes, his own full of the surging emotions he had no idea how to voice.

She smiled with contentment and squeezed his hand.

He squeezed back, and when her gaze left his, he turned his head and looked down at his wife.

Bridget had both lips pulled between her teeth and her eyes were shining.

"If she gets to call you Daddy, I want to, too." Portia's lip came out, but her eyes were worried, like she might not be as important.

"Please. I would consider it an honor for you to call me Daddy." His words were true, if a bit choked up.

"And me?" Robin asked, her words more guarded.

"You, too." He took a breath. "Man, you girls sure know how to squeeze a man's heart." It hurt a little in the best possible way – pain because they had to suffer loss for him to be standing here, but everything else was pure pleasure.

They got their hot chocolates, walking along the sidewalk, enjoying the town's Christmas decorations and each other's company. He had a lot of great memories of his family growing up, but walking with his new family in his new hometown with the magic of Christmas in the air all around them had to be one of the best.

Maybe not the exact best, he thought, later than night as he lay curled up with his wife, warm and content to his soul.

"Shawn?" she asked, sleepily.

"Hmm?" he said, running a hand down her soft arm and over her stomach.

"I saw you talking to Drake and Ralph when the girls and I were coming back from the restroom. What did they say?"

He hesitated. If there was anything in his life that wasn't perfect, it was this.

"You don't have to tell me," she finally said, but there was disappointment in her voice.

"I just...I feel bad because I said I would convince the town the curse was bogus and...I don't like not being able to keep my word."

"You've done everything you can."

"I know. He said I was 'lucky' that the tractor didn't kill me and I might not be so 'lucky' next time."

"Oh," she whispered. His words had upset her, like he'd known they would. "What did you say?" she asked after a small silence.

"That I didn't believe in luck. That anything good that happened to me was because of His providence and anything bad was allowed by His hand, too. I guess I can't browbeat the truth into anyone's head, but sometimes I want to."

"Me, too." She sighed. "I'm sorry they're still bothering you."

"I'm just sorry it bothers you."

"It doesn't. Not anymore, because you're right. I actually see it as a good thing because it's forced our family to band together. It's kind of like it's us against them, even though I love my town and the people in it. If that makes sense?"

"It does." He brushed his lips over the hair at her temple. "Thank you for taking a chance on me. No matter what God allows into our future, you're the best thing that ever happened to me."

"Hmm. Really?" She stretched and he moved with her. "Maybe rather than telling me, I'd prefer you show me."

"I can do that, Hon." He trailed his lips down to the corner of her jaw. "Happily."

Epilogue

B raxton Emerson tapped a finger on the table. There were no lights on in his kitchen, and his daughter was sleeping upstairs.

He'd always been comfortable in the dark. He'd always been comfortable alone, as well. He'd also always been comfortable being in charge, commanding, leading his brothers, and being responsible for making decisions that could impact whether or not their farm prospered or failed.

What he wasn't comfortable with was being in the city. Being around a lot of people. Conforming to rules and regulations that didn't make any sense to him and didn't benefit society.

But Arian's mother had texted him for the first time since she'd gotten out of prison and asked to see her daughter. She'd specifically asked if he could bring her or send her to Toronto, where she was working.

The text had come in two days ago, and he hadn't answered it yet.

He had zero desire to leave the country. And even less to send his daughter abroad.

But he didn't want to be unreasonable.

He'd been trying to figure out a compromise. One that would work for both of them, and he hadn't been able to think of anything.

Still, Christmas was coming, and as Arian had done every year since he'd brought her home with him, she'd asked to see her mother for Christmas.

He'd like to be able to give that to her.

But he wasn't going to go to Toronto to do it. He needed a passport, for one. And he wouldn't have that before Christmas.

Then, an idea so brilliant, so amazing, so perfect he couldn't believe he hadn't thought of it before, popped into his head, and he gave himself a half a second to allow his lips to relax into an almost smile, before he pulled out his phone and wrote a text.

Enjoy this preview of *Heartland Cheer*, just for you!

Heartland Cheer

Chapter 1

"Do you see Mom?" Arian asked, straining to look through the group of people who had congregated at the edge of the Niagara River, eager to see the fascinating and beautiful light display that was put on every night as the water in the river rushed over the falls, creating one of the most stunning displays of power and of God's amazing handiwork on the continent.

It might be the beginning of December, but it was unseasonably warm, and Braxton Emerson wore a T-shirt and jeans.

It had been all over the local news about the unseasonably warm fall this area had had.

Being from Iowa, Braxton hadn't had a clue what the local weather was doing until he'd arrived earlier this afternoon.

He and Arian had checked into their rented house, then Arian could barely contain herself, wanting to see the falls for the first time in her life.

The first time she could remember.

"She might not be here," he said. "We're not supposed to meet until nine o'clock, and that's at the lobby of the hotel where she's staying."

"She's going to come to our house?" Arian asked, even though she'd already asked that question and he'd answered the same way he was going to answer now.

"I don't know."

When she was younger, Arian hadn't been a big talker, but over the last year or so, there'd been a lot of changes happening, both in her body and her personality.

As a single dad, he hadn't felt prepared to deal with any of those changes.

Maybe that was part of the reason he'd gone out of his way to meet his wife.

She wasn't his ex. He'd never wanted a divorce, and she'd never asked for one.

No one had known about their marriage anyway.

Tempted to finger the chain around his neck on which his wedding band hung, he didn't. It was tucked under his T-shirt, and maybe he was a sentimental fool, but he never took it off.

"The hydroelectric power plant located just upstream was at one time the largest hydroelectric power plant in the world." The tour guide's voice of the tour group standing slightly in front of him droned on.

Braxton wasn't really paying attention, although he did find the falls fascinating. This wasn't his first time here, and some of the happiest, and saddest, moments of his life had been spent here.

He hadn't thought he'd ever come back.

"At this time of year, the Niagara River is already at its lowest seasonal level, and about seventy-five percent of the river is diverted at night to feed the turbines of the power plant."

After the guide said this, there was murmuring in the group, as people were astonished that so much of the river was diverted. It didn't really take away from the beauty of the falls nor the power that a person felt as the ground vibrated from the surge beating as the water landed far below.

"How deep is the river now?" one lady asked. Braxton found himself looking over the railing, wondering that himself.

"It's approximately two feet deep," the guide said with confidence. "In some places, it's less and others, more. But don't let the shallowness fool you. The current is still strong and swift and moving quite quickly."

He went on to talk about the speed of the water and the force of the current, and Braxton quit listening, thinking about his daughter and wondering if this was the best thing for her.

He was only spending two weeks here, and he'd be back in Iowa for Christmas. Krista, his wife, had asked for Christmas with her daughter, and he'd compromised by saying that he would come the whole way to Niagara Falls, which made her trip from Toronto short and easy, and she would be able to spend almost all of her break with her daughter.

In return, Christmas would be as it always was for them, at the big old farmhouse in Iowa, with his brothers and grandmother.

Maybe it was selfish of him to want that tradition to be unbroken, but he'd spent five years away from home, and he'd sworn when he went back that he'd never leave it again.

The group moved a little farther away, and the sound of the pounding water drowned out any more of their conversation. He and Arian needed to make their way up as well, since the hotel they were meeting Krista at was farther upriver.

He started to walk, and his daughter fell into step beside him. They went slowly, both of them fascinated by the water and the power it represented.

It was hard to imagine a more beautiful night to be out, although the warmth of the evening probably made it more crowded than it might normally be.

Nervous anticipation curled in his stomach, and he could feel adrenaline pushing through his veins, making him want to run. Whether it would be toward his wife or away from her, he wasn't sure.

Equal parts of both, probably.

Arian and he had strolled for probably ten minutes, stopping every once in a while when they came to a spot where the railing was clear to step closer and stare at the silent but swiftly moving river.

They were stopped at a random spot when a woman ahead of them caught his eye.

It wasn't the woman exactly, at first anyway, but it was more the dog she carried.

It looked familiar, and a memory he hadn't thought of in a decade slammed into him so hard he put a hand on the railing.

"Dad?" Arian said, concern darkening her deep brown eyes.

He shook his head. "I'm fine," he said, summoning up just a bit of a smile. As the oldest of four brothers, he wasn't used to showing weakness.

Plus, the one time he allowed his defenses to come down and gave his heart to someone, she'd broken it, quite brutally, and thrown it back at him.

No. Weakness wasn't something he was good at.

The people around them shifted, and he saw the dog again.

The woman holding it was slender and tall, both of which were emphasized by the long, tailored pants she wore and the stylish and snug-fitting sweater.

The dog seemed restless, squirming in her arms as the woman stood at the rail, turned just enough upriver that he couldn't see the outline of her features but could watch the wind lifting her hair and blowing it back away from her face.

The dog wriggled again, seeming to squirm almost to get out of her arms, and she shifted, as though she were preoccupied.

He supposed it could be Krista, and the thought made him stop a good hundred feet back.

Surely not.

Back when he knew her, she'd never been early for anything in her life, and it was at least an hour until they were to meet.

The dog...

It reminded him so much of Cricket, the dog he'd bought her as a wedding gift.

Maybe it seemed like a strange gift, but they'd been driving in the Finger Lakes and had stopped at an Amish fruit market to buy some apples. There had been several Amish children running around the yard playing with puppies, adorable and sweet, innocent and cute.

Those puppies happened to be for sale.

Krista had been charmed, and he'd been completely and totally under her spell. He would have said yes to anything, but she hadn't had to ask.

They'd just looked at each other and known. And they'd spent the rest of their honeymoon with the puppy.

Because of Krista's upbringing, bouncing from one foster care home to another, she'd fallen deeply and irrevocably in love with the dog. Even the birth of their daughter a year later hadn't dethroned Cricket from her place in Krista's heart.

It had been one of the things he'd loved about her. Her capacity to love, deeply and without restraint. Freely and beautifully and fearlessly.

The opposite of him, really. The opposite in that Krista loved everything and everyone that way.

Braxton only loved Krista and his family with that kind of dangerous love.

The crowd shifted again, and this time, he spent such an obviously long amount of time staring that Arian turned her head and looked as well.

"That looks like the dog I had when I was little," she murmured, possibly putting the idea that that could be her mother together in her brain.

She didn't say. She just let the sentence end abruptly.

Pick up your copy of Heartland Cheer by Jessie Gussman today!

A Gift from Jessie

View this code through your smart phone camera to be taken to a page where you can download a FREE ebook when you sign up to get updates from Jessie Gussman! Find out why people say, "Jessie's is the only newsletter I open and read" and "You make my day brighter. Love, love, love reading your newsletters. I don't know where you find time to write books. You are so busy living life. A true blessing." and "I know from now on that I can't be drinking my morning coffee while reading your newsletter – I laughed so hard I sprayed it out all over the table!"

Made in the USA
Columbia, SC
05 February 2023

11516690R00098